I0536297

Countess who Kissed a Count

Seasons Bliss Series

IreAnne Chambers

Published by Purple Storm Publishing, 2024.

This is a work of fiction. Similarities to real people, places, or events are entirely coincidental.

COUNTESS WHO KISSED A COUNT

First edition. October 30, 2024.

Copyright © 2024 IreAnne Chambers.

ISBN: 978-0996414692

Written by IreAnne Chambers.

Table of Contents

To the family I love both in the U.S. and in Greece
and my best friends of forever.

SOME MOMENTS ARE FLEETING, BUT SOME... THEY LINGER FOREVER

When Lady Evangeline "Eva" Diamandis, the enigmatic Countess of Tripolia, arrives in the heart of Cleveland, Ohio, she expects a brief escape with her friend, Naz. But life—and love—often have plans of their own. At a quaint autumn corn maze, she stumbles into the most unexpected encounter.

Sebastian "Bo" MacLachlan, a local artist and country singer, moonlights at a corn maze to help a friend. In a moment steeped in the scent of cider and the allure of October mystery, Eva and Bo share a kiss that blurs the lines and crosses boundaries.

Eva's heart is divided, tied to a life of duty in her Mediterranean homeland of Thalassia. Bo, with his paint-streaked hands and soulful songs, represents everything she's never known—authentic, simple, raw. For Bo, Eva is an inspiration, a portrait of beauty and grace that demands to be immortalized.

Their lives take a spiral neither saw coming.

Immerse yourself in a love story that spans continents, defies social boundaries, and reminds us that sometimes, the path to true love isn't just twisted—it's royal, rugged, and endlessly romantic.

AUTHOR'S NOTE

Confession time. As many of my readers and friends may know, I'm not a fan of Halloween celebrations. That said, I decided to included two scenes that include a true life recollection of something I experienced when I was a young adult. Since it is based on a true life experience, I decided to go ahead and put it into the story because it is one-of-a-kind and an experience I consider unique. I wanted to make sure those of you who may feel the same about Halloween know, in case this may be triggering.

The characters and events portrayed in this book are fictitious or are used fictitiously. Any similarity to real persons, living or dead, is purely coincidental and not intended by the author.

CHAPTER ONE

In the Fall, Cleveland, Ohio

E very. Single. Day. The same question. Every. Single. Day. Eva opens her eyes and stares at the white swirl design on the ceiling. She turns her head to look out the window that encompasses the entire wall of the bedroom. Nothing but sky. A blue sky. A blue sky with swirls of white clouds not unlike the ceiling swirls. Eva wallows and sinks down into the white comforter. How much more can she take?

Paparazzi. George. Parents. The world. "With privilege comes responsibility." Eva's sick of hearing it. If the Royal Family in London can change, why can't hers? Eva inhales a deep cleansing breath and counts until she can breathe no longer. One, two...ten. Exhale... slow counts back down. Why does she keep doing this exercise? It doesn't work. It never works. Anxiety never goes away. Coming to America to visit Naz is supposed to help. It hasn't.

Eva throws off the covers and sits up. George is probably up already. The man hardly sleeps. At least he allows her personal space. Separate bedrooms since the honeymoon. Naz has three bedrooms in her Downtown Cleveland condo. Perfect for her situation. Eva walks to the balcony and opens the door. Chilly air comes off the water. People are already out running around the waterfront of the park. People are fishing. People are even playing volleyball in the sand courts.

October isn't this cold in Tripolia. Goosebumps break out on Eva's arm and she rubs each arm up and down in unison. Over the balcony the Great Lake of Erie lays. An ocean. Reminiscent of home. The only thing missing is Thalassia's salty sea air. Eva leans over the rail to see what's below. Silent waves collide against the boat dock. Another deep breath before walking inside. The reflective glass door reveals a hive of mussed up hair. Time to ask Naz where the best place is to get highlights touched up. The Countess of Tripolia can't walk around like a punked-out skunk. A minute in front of the mirror is more than enough for one day. The person staring back has been forged that way. Lady Evangeline Diamandis. Eva unwinds the purple lock of hair carefully tucked behind her ear so that it blows with the wind. There. That's better.

Fried bacon. The smell wafts through the hall. Hunger gurgles in Eva's stomach. She follows the smell to the kitchen. Typical. George is reading a paper at the table. Eva takes a seat next to him and squints to see the letters. Crap. She left her contacts in her room. Not only is everything blurred, but amber eyes will have to be visible until blue eyes can be tapped in.

"Eva, you're awake! Sleep well?" Naz dances in the kitchen to Bollywood's Indian music while she cooks. Perky Naz, always bouncing around to some kind of music in the morning, always into the latest musical performance from her country.

"I'm good." Eva rubs her eyes. The plate Naz sets on the table is blurred turquoise with brown strips and a yellow-gold eye surrounded by white.

2

"Aw, come on. It's not that bad. What's wrong?"

"Nothing. You just reminded me of my first night at Oxford."

"I fixed you bacon and eggs?"

"I wish." Naz watches Eva fill her cup three quarters of the way with cream and then add coffee.

"I forgot you do that."

"Do what?"

"Literally add coffee to your milk."

"Oh that." Evan slurps a full mouth of her just-the-way-I-like-it java fix. Perfect temperature. "And you don't remember getting up at five in the morning every day to sing to your '*tweety* bird?'"

"Oh my! Tweety bird! He was the best parakeet I ever had."

Eva scans the room. "Don't tell me you have another one?"

"Another tweety bird? No. No time. This lawyering business keeps me on my toes if you haven't noticed."

One bite of the bacon and all the day's worries subside. Savory and delicious. Eggs are good too, but so much better with bacon. Naz has always been so thoughtful. Even if bacon isn't her first choice for breakfast or anything, for that matter. "Are you sure it's not too much having us stay with you? Filling all your extra space? Making you cook meat even though you're a vegetarian?"

"You? Of course not. I know I don't have to babysit you. And, you know I would do anything for my good friends. But, I do have plans for you today."

"Oh?" Eva gulps down more of her java fix.

"Yep. We're going to do something impulsive. Something I'm sure you've never done in that backwoods country of yours."

"Backwoods? Not quite. Better watch what you say, or I might have to take to social media like your politicians do."

Naz's laugh reminds Eva of a time before her life exploded into shrapnel. "You would never last a minute on social media."

"True." Social media and I are not friends. "So what is it?"

"Somewhere you can lose your security detail."

"I like it already. Tell me more."

"Ever heard of a corn maze?"

George puts down the paper, pulls his plate closer, and picks up his fork. "What's that you say?"

BO PULLS HIS CHEVY Silverado into the grass lot next to Don's old farmhouse. Each year it's more weathered and more worn. Fresh cut hay and horse manure drift over into the cab area as soon as the door opens. Stalks of dried corn remain after the harvest and the opening to the maze has been plowed through in three directions. Stair-stacked bails frame three scarecrow crosses. People are going to scream tonight when they realize the scarecrows are alive.

"Bastian! We need you over here."

A pumpkin-lined path to the barn ends with Jimmy sorting through costumes. "It's Bo, remember?" Jimmy's focus is on the outfits in front of him, unaware of anything else going on around him. Volunteering to help at the corn maze festival tonight will have its challenges. No doubt. If not for the kids... home working on his new riff is where Bo prefers to be. Bo hums the lyrics of his new song.

"Okay, yeah. Bo." Jimmy tosses Bo a stack of costumes. Yep, riffs. Much better use of his time.

"How do you get Bo from Sebastian?"

Bo takes the mound of clothes. "Does it matter? It's just Bo. I don't call you Jamie, do I?" Bo's not in the mood to go into why his parents named him Sebastian.

Jimmy shakes his head and continues sorting through hangers of wardrobe items. "Pass those out and come back. I'm almost done with yours."

"Mine? I'm not dressing up. Don told me I was at the door tonight." Traipsing through a corn maze trying to scare people is not on Bo's agenda tonight.

Jimmy nods in the direction of the entrance to the barn. "Just go pass them out and come back. I'll talk to Don."

A group of kids languish near the barn doors, weaving in and out between each other, laughing and goofing off. Bo hums his new song again. The vibration rings in his ears and keeps him from spelling out what he'd like to say to dear old "Jamie." Gotta set a good example. He tosses each of the kids their garb and heads back to Jimmy in time to see two more kids carrying out a wooden box.

"How's it look?"

"What is it?"

"Your coffin." Jimmy hands Bo a black silk cape, black sweat pants, and a tuxedo t-shirt.

"My what?"

Don's wife, Greta, walks in, shoves Bo down in a chair, and unzips a makeup bag that she then plops down on the table next to him. "No. Not happening. Absolutely not."

"Sorry, hon. Don says we need you for this." Greta tosses his Stetson hat on the table beside him, shoves back his head, and starts to apply white.

Jimmy scrounges in a plastic bag. Plastic fangs slide across the same table. "Count Dracula can't be without his teeth."

Humming isn't going to cut it this time.

COUNTESS WHO KISSED A COUNT

CHAPTER TWO

Eva can't breathe. The limo is stifling. George must have the heat up to eighty degrees. She searches her bag for the Chinese fan always flattened on the bottom. Nothing. She needs something to help circulate the air in front of her face. Eva looks up at Naz's friend Dialah. Her cheeks are pink. Naz has beads of sweat on her forehead. Eva cracks the window waiting for George's reprimand. She knows it's coming. She doesn't care. Fresh air and highway. Much better.

"Eva, really? Must you?"

"Yes, I must. We're warm blooded creatures, George. You're cooking us to a crisp."

"Eva, it must be close to zero outside. I can't abide it. Close the window."

"It's nowhere near zero." Eva looks at Naz. "What does your phone say?"

Naz picks up her phone. "Sixty degrees." She taps it closed and puts it face down in her palm.

"There. See?"

George glares at Naz. Naz looks out the window. Dialah stares at her lap. Dialah doesn't say much. Probably afraid.

"Eva, don't make me ask the driver to lock the controls."

Must every sentence start with her name? Eva can't "abide" that. She ignores him and presses her face out the window to feel the air. He's not going to roll it up while her face is in the way.

"Driver! The window, please."

"Wait." The window slides up. "No!" Eva slips her face back and out of the way, but her hair gets tangled. "Now, look what you've done!" She tugs her head to show "his lordship."

George knocks on the glass separating the front from the back. "Driver." The window slides down, releases Eva's hair, and up it goes again. Glip, glip. Locked.

Black, horn-rimmed, glasses are directed at her along with a tight-lipped, smug smile. Eva wants to throttle him. Horn-rimmed glasses and all. She needs out. Now. The burn inside her stomach begins to singe. Naz tries to help settle things. "We're almost there. It's the next exit, and then only a short distance down the road."

The driver pulls into a driveway that leads to an open field with some parked cars. The limo stops. Eva tries to open the door to get out. Crap. Still locked.

"Eva..." Eva glares at the man sitting across from her and dares him to say another word. He doesn't.

Naz does instead. "Why don't Dialah and I hop out and get tickets while you two wait here? Let your security scope things out first. What do you think?"

Perfect. Eva folds her arms across her chest and bites the inside of her cheeks. Leaving her with him is a sure way to help her calm down. Said no one.

"Good idea." George doesn't get it. He never gets it. The whole section of their wedding ceremony where counsel was given on how to treat your wife, lost. Completely lost. Naz and Dialah get out. Eva sits back, takes a deep breath, and counts.

"Eva..."

"Ten, nine..." Eva closes her eyes.

"Eva?"

"One." She opens her eyes. "What?" She doesn't want to see the man's face. Blurred vision is what she wants right now. Why couldn't she have forgotten to wear them?

"I think it might be best if I sit in the car and wait for you. It's too cold."

Eva couldn't be more pleased.

"You'll have fun with your friends." George's condescending, I-always-know-best, smile irritates her. It irritates even more because he's right.

His one wise thought of the day. "Whatever." Eva opens the door to step out. Nothing. She's surrounded by nothing. Complete darkness except for flood lights around the entrance. And then horses. Their mossy smell and the moon. A moon so bright the expanse of the field is lit up by its luminescence. A few people walk into a barn. Eva looks up. A star-filled sky expands across the heavens. The singe from earlier wastes away in the heavy, dark, quiet. Naz hands Eva her ticket.

Naz and Dialah look up too. Naz's warm hand resonates on Eva's forearm. "What is it?"

"This is the first time I can remember stepping into nothing."

"What do you mean?"

"No flashes. No screaming. No chasing. No one is here."

"Ah. About that. There might be screaming. And chasing. And flashes." Naz repositions herself between Dialah and Eva. She links their arms and escorts them to the entrance. "But I doubt anyone would expect the Countess of Tripoli to venture out into a corn maze in the middle of the night. And I dare your security to follow us."

"What do you mean, screaming?"

Naz lets go and jogs into the stalks of corn and disappears. Dialah goes next. What are they doing? It's dark and hard to see. What did Naz mean when she said there would be screaming?

"Wait! Naz? Dialah?"

Screams and giggles echo through the maze of the moonlit corn field. Flashing lights cast lanky shadows of distorted corn stalks. Eva waves her hands in front of her to try and stay on the path. There are lights ahead.

"Raaar!" The loud scream shocks and surprises Eva. She screams back at the bloody face next to her shoulder. What the—? Eva starts laughing. Probably not the reaction they're hoping for. She can't help it. Emotional overload.

Naz and Dialah yell out from ahead. Eva picks up her pace. "Naz, wait for me!"

"Hurry up! No way we're coming back there. We'll see you at the end."

Great. Some friend. Eva doesn't blame her. Naz lives for this kind of thing. Eva? Not so much.

"Boo!" Eva stares at the short little "thing" with cloth over its head and two cut out eye holes. Not very impressive. Little thing points in the direction of a tall box and then runs away. Eva starts another round of laughing. Why not? Let's see what's over there. Lights flash, voices moan. Eva laughs. The door opens. Eva trips.

She trips right into the arms of Count Dracula himself. So close. So close to his face. The color of his blue eyes glow, even in the dark moonlight. White face. Red lips. His hands are now firm around Eva's waist. It's been too long. Too long since she's been this close to a man. Eva leans into him. Unable to stop. She doesn't want to stop. His lips hover inches from hers. Close. Mint breath tickles the side of her cheek, close. Eva taps the corner of his mouth with her lips. What is she doing? His response is an instant full-on-the-mouth kiss. A tongue touching, jet-engines-hitting-turbulence kiss. Eva's engines haven't had turbulence like this in a long time. She wraps her arms around his neck and he pulls her in. The door to the coffin shuts. Muffled voices scream outside. Who cares? All that matters right now is what this man is doing. Kissing her. Kissing her like he knows what she wants. Kissing her like she's a woman he can't get enough of. Kissing her.

"Eva! Where are you?"

The seat belt sign on Eva's private jet turns off. "I need to go." George calls out again. His voice, closer this time. Eva drops her hands to her side and waits for Count Dracula to open the coffin door. Her eyes are fastened to his. She wants to remember the kindness and warmth of them. And the feels. Cool air grazes her back. The Count still doesn't speak. Eva stands on her tiptoes and bestows one last kiss on the corner of his mouth and then turns in the direction of George's voice.

George is standing next to the scarecrows at the entrance. It must be the exit too. "What took you so long? And what's all over your face?"

"What do you mean?" Eva wipes her mouth and cheek with the back of her hand. White. "Oh, that. Just something I ran into."

George looks at his watch. "Naz and Dialah are already in the car. I've been standing out here in the cold for an hour."

"I'm sure it hasn't been an hour."

"It has been." George grabs Eva's arm to direct her to the car. Enough. She has had enough. Eva jerks her arm away.

"Nobody asked you to stand out here."

"What?" George reaches out for her arm again.

She moves to avoid him. "In fact, you didn't even have to come if you thought it was too cold for your wellbeing." Eva's voice escalates into a yell. She doesn't care.

"Eva..."

"Stop calling me Eva!"

"Eva..." George removes his glasses, pinches the bridge of nose, closes his eyes, and breaths in. Like *he's* the one who needs a cleansing breath. "That *is* your name."

"Raaaar!"

Eva's yell morphs into a scream. Two scarecrows jump down from the bales of hay at the same time. One on each side. Eva laughs. George doesn't. Count Dracula walks out the exit of the maze.

George fixates on Dracula. George's mouth opens like he wants to speak, but nothing comes out. Something's off. One eye droops, one side of his jaw sags. His words slur nonsense. Eva's stomach suddenly feels empty. She closes the gap between them, reaching out to hold his elbow as he begins to sink. "What is it? George, what's wrong?" One side of his body goes limp and he falls to the ground.

Count Dracula yells across the yard. "Call 911!"

"IS THAT HER?" DON WALKS into Bo's studio-garage and hands him a cup of coffee.

"Thanks." Bo opens the lid to look in. Black. Just what he needs. He steps back and studies the portrait outlined on canvas. Her features etched in pencil before they become lost in a memory. Bo sips. Scorching liquid drips down his throat. He breathes in and out fast to cool it.

"Be careful, it's hot." Don's smile is hidden behind his mustache, but Bo knows it's there.

Idiot. Why do people feel they need to state the obvious? "You think?"

"Did you find out who she is?"

"Yes." Bo blows the edge of his cup and inhales Starbuck's dark roast before trying to sip again. Better. He taps the canvas to adjust the shape of the corners to her eyes. Amber? It was dark. He wants to see those eyes again. He wants to see her again.

"Well, are you going to tell me?"

"Tell you what?"

"Who she is."

"You probably wouldn't believe me."

"Try me."

"She's the Countess of Tripoli. Eva Diamantis."

"The what?" Don chokes his laugh out mid-sip. "How did you find out?"

"I asked their driver."

Don settles. "I guess he would know. Any news on how her father is?"

"No. I think I might go to the Cleveland Clinic and visit."

"Oh, so you found out what hospital he's at."

Bo picks up a rag and throws it at Don's face. It hits the mark. "I heard the paramedics, you idiot. You know I have an aversion to news outlets."

Bo drinks his coffee and stares at the creation in front of him. It's almost perfect. Cheekbones need work. Bo rubs at the paint on his hands. Hands that touched those cheekbones when he kissed her. Hands that want to touch her again. In more places. For longer.

"I wouldn't."

"Wouldn't what?"

"Go to the Clinic."

"Well, I'm not you."

"Seriously, man. Do you think you'll even get near her again? With her security?"

"Won't know until I try."

"Did you Google her?"

"No, I didn't *Google* her."

"You should. See what she's all about."

"No. I'll see what she's all about up close."

"Riiight. Don't say I didn't warn you, bro." Don sips his coffee and coughs.

Bo shakes his head. Don can be a real butthead, for lack of a more elegant description.

"In fact, I think I'm gonna go now." Bo throws his brushes into a bin and leaves them to soak in water.

"Want me to come with?" Bo pulls out one of his cloth handkerchiefs to dry his hands.

"No."

"Okay, if you're sure."

"I'm sure." Don gets in his truck to leave. "Come over for a beer later."

"We'll see." All Bo wants right now is to get to the hospital and see her again. To find out how she's doing. He dons his Stetson, hops in his truck, and drives as fast as he can without running any lights, hands off to the valets, and get directions to the floor where they're at. The VIP wing. Will he get through? Don's words echo in his head.

Bo steps off the elevator and two men in black suits step in front of him. He clears his throat hoping to sound more confident. "I'd like to see the Countess."

"I'm sorry, sir. You'll have to leave."

Bo looks around and over them. She's right there, down the hall. One of the girls from last night is with her talking with the doctor. What happened? She's crying. Bo pushes through the two men in black when they turn to see. One strong arm slaps him on the shoulder to pull him back. Eva looks up in his direction.

"It's okay. Let him come." Bo watches her fall back into her friend's arms and cry.

What can he say? He takes off his Stetson and makes a short ruffle through the top of his hair to reshape it. He wants to be near her. Touch her. Hold her. Comfort her.

Her friend holds out her hand. "I'm Naz."

"Bo."

Eva doesn't stop crying. Naz guides her to a chair to sit. "Shh. It's gonna be okay."

Bo sits down on the other side and places his hat on the chair next to him. What can he do? What can he say? He feels around in his pockets to offer her a handkerchief or tissue or something. Naz does instead. "How is he?"

"He had a stroke." Eva sniffs, takes a deep breath, and closes her eyes.

Bo waits.

"He didn't wake up." She starts crying again. "He's not going to wake up." Her words trail off.

Instinctively, Bo puts his arm around her shoulder and she leans against him. "I'm sorry. I'm sorry this happened to you."

"I don't even know why I'm crying. It's not as if we had the best relationship."

"I'm sure your father knew you loved him. Parents know these things." Eva sits up and stops crying. Her olive skin is blotched with red patches. Her brows push together, confused. Worried. What did he say? What worried her?

She turns around to face forward and twirls the tissue between her fingers. A strand of hair dangles along the side of her face. Purple? Bo needs to add that to her portrait. "He wasn't my father."

"Uncle?"

"Try again."

COUNTESS WHO KISSED A COUNT

CHAPTER THREE

"**A**re you sure this is what you want?" Eva watches Bo hand the valet ticket to the attendant. She nods her head. Words are stuck to the roof of her mouth. Controlled breathing isn't helping. Counting isn't helping. Too many things roil in her brain. Shock, relief, guilt. The empty sickness in the trench called her stomach will not ease. Panic threatens. Eva wants out. Out of this hospital. Out of life as she knows it. Away from the last three years. Away from him. Away from George.

The valet attendant hands Bo the key and he helps Eva up into his truck. Bo places his hand on the small of her back like it belongs there. He steadies her, guides her, helps her up. He waits between the truck and the door while she settles in. "Where do you want to go?"

Blurred confusion rages like foam at the bottom of a waterfall. Eva takes a deep breath to try and defog the mist. "I don't know." Anxiety percolates, ready to crush her. "I don't care. Can we just drive?"

"Driving, it is." Bo closes her door and gets in the driver's side. He puts the truck in gear. Eva watches the muscles in his forearm flex with each movement. George would never agree so easy to something she wanted to do. There it is again. Guilt. Eva looks out the window. Buildings. Houses. Parks. People.

Highway. The heavy silence hypnotizes. Acceleration onto the entrance ramp shoves her back in her seat. George would never approve. Wetness pools under her eyes. It's been years since she's been in the front seat of any vehicle. And next to a man she's actually attracted to. A man she only knows as Bo. A man she recognized from the moment he stepped out of the elevator. More guilt. Will it ever go away?

Bo opens a compartment between the seats and hands her the last tissue in the box.

"Is there anything I can do? Are you hungry?"

Eva looks over at Bo. Blond curls edge the line below the rim of his hat. He glances her way for a second. "I guess I could eat."

"Perfect." He gets off the highway at the next exit and pulls into a parking spot on the street that someone just pulled out of. "I hope you like Greek."

"As a matter of fact, George and I had Greek in New York City. We eat Greek food often." Does he know where she's from?

"Hmm." Bo puts his truck in reverse. "Are you sure? There are plenty of choices."

"It's fine. Greek is fine."

Bo hops out, walks around to her side, and opens the door. He offers his hand to help her down. His firm grip wraps around her fingers. Protective. Memories of the corn maze push forward. Tears threaten to break through. Guilt burns in her chest. George would never...George is dead. Who is she crying for? George or for herself?

BO WATCHES EVA'S FACIAL expressions. Grim and gray, as she moves with grace. Eva places her hand in his to allow him to help her down from his truck. "This place is probably not as fancy as you're used to, but they have good food. I know you'll like it."

"I'm sure it's fine." Her voice cracks. There is a slight moisture forming around her eyes.

"What can I do to help?"

"What?"

"You're upset."

"Of course, I am. My husband just died and part of me can't accept it happened while another part feels like I'm finally free from a loveless marriage— " Eva covers her mouth while a tear works its way down her cheek. "I can't believe I said that. I've never said that." She turns her face away. "I did love him."

"Of course you did. He was your husband."

"I mean, ours *was* an arranged marriage. And, it was difficult. I complained. He complained. I got upset. He got upset. I only wanted more freedom." Eva's voice changes from a low murmur to a hush and then drops into a quick and dead silence. "But, I did love him. And I believe he loved me."

"Listen, I haven't been married. Yes, I'm a thirty-two year-old bachelor." Why did he feel the need to state the obvious? Bo turns her to face him. "But, I've had relationships before. It's normal to have conflict. I have no doubt you loved him."

"But, what if I didn't love him enough? What if I caused this because of my wants? What if something out there said, 'okay, here you go?'"

More tears fall and Eva wipes them away with her fingertips. Bo pulls her to the side, away from the foot traffic of the sidewalk. Each swipe of Eva's finger tips draws his attention. Each swipe accentuates a well-manicured nail design. A dominant color of medium dusty blue, reminiscent of the domed rooftops of the Santorini Island photos of the Mediterranean, not unlike colors used in Bo's latest piece of art.

"If you're saying you think you caused this because of some wish or prayer, then stop it. The world doesn't work that way. Things sometimes just *happen*. That's it. That's the way life is. Unforeseen occurrences." What else can he say? She needs to feel better. She needs to come to terms with what's happening. Loss of this magnitude is not something everyone experiences early in life. Before one has had a chance to experience life together. One thing is sure. Eva is not responsible for George's death. "Wait here for a minute."

Bo jogs back to his truck to grab a tissue. The box is empty. He grabs some napkins from the glove box instead. He turns back to Eva and sees the tears streaming down her face again. He makes his way back to her and hands her a napkin. "I'm sorry, this is all I have."

Eva takes it and begins dabbing at the corners of her eyes. "It's okay. I think society is past gentlemen carrying embroidered handkerchiefs."

Bo holds back smiling, too broadly. He does still carry cloth handkerchiefs when he is painting. Maybe he needs to think about embroidering them. How can he bring her spirits back up? He does the only thing he can think of to do. She is royalty, right? He bows in front of her waving his right arm diagonally across his chest. "My Lady, forgive the impropriety..." Bo peeks up at Eva from his lowered position. He can see the small, upturned curve of her lips so he continues. "...my butler neglected to refill my pocket with a clean cloth this morning. You can be sure he will receive the requisite scolding."

Eva's smile spills into a small giggle. "Your butler? I didn't know men in the Americas had use for such positions in their households."

"Of course, we do. How else would single men of moderate means survive?" Single men of moderate means? Where did that come from? He must have heard something along those lines somewhere in his English Literature class from his college days. At least that makes some kind of sense.

"If you say so." Eva holds her chin up in mock pride.

Bo chooses to take her playful pride attempt as a positive reaction to his somewhat lame attempt at humor. What's got into him? He never allows women to make him squirm. Eva is different. He knew this the moment she fell into his arms at the corn maze. "Maybe the term 'butler' needs replaced with 'mother' or maybe a cleaning lady."

"That's more closer to the truth, I think." Eva half smiles. At least the tears have faded.

Bo looks down at their interlocking fingers. He's caressing the tops of her hands with his thumbs. When did he take her hands in his? Instinct must have kicked in during his efforts to console her and make her laugh. The quietness between them grows more intense. Bo can't help but stare at Eva's solemn face.

She glances up from their shared silence. "I'm sorry. I don't think I can go in to eat. I don't even feel very hungry right now. Can you take me back to my friend's condo? It's a short distance from the Rock Hall of Fame, I think is what it's called." Eva pulls her hands from his soft grip.

"Eva, you have to eat. Let's just go in." Bo locks his hands in his front pockets and gestures with his shoulders toward the entrance. "If all you want is a coffee, or wine, or beer...or anything, it's fine. But, why not try and eat something?" He doesn't want their evening to end.

Eva's eyes begin to gloss over again. "No, I think it best I go."

Bo contemplates what to say next. He doesn't want to push too hard, if for no other reason than he believes she shouldn't be alone right now. Or maybe it's him? He wants to pull her close and make it all go away, but he holds himself back. It will have to wait. Eva needs time. Only time can help with this kind of loss. Isn't that what everyone says?

COUNTESS WHO KISSED A COUNT

CHAPTER FOUR

"She gave you her number, broh. What are you waiting for? Just call her." Don takes a gulp of his Killian's Irish Red. Bo stares back. Don's in one of his college boy moods. Sometimes it's funny, sometimes it's not. Today Bo's leaning towards not.

Bo contemplates how to make the call. He's been contemplating for days. Bo crosses his legs at his ankles and leans back in his chair with his hands behind his head. "It's not that easy, *Broh*."

Don chuffs out another sound and shakes his head. "Just call her, dude. Here, I'll dial the number." Don holds out his arm and backward-waves in Bo's direction. "Give me your phone." Don repeats the backward-wave. "Come on." Don takes another chug of his beer.

Bo slaps down Don's hand and matches his tone. "Nah, man. I can call her myself."

"Well then, get on with it. She could be leaving." Don bends his arm back to his chest.

"Don. You know cell phones work anywhere, right?"

"Yeah, but you want to see her, don't you?"

Bo knows Don is right. "Of course I want to see her."

"Well then?"

Bo picks up a pillow and throws it at his friend's head. It hits its mark and knocks Don's baseball hat to the floor. "What the... Why? Just why?"

"Because."

Don stands up, picks up his hat and repositions it back on his head. "I think my job is done here."

"Your job?"

"Yeah. I gotta get home for dinner or Greta will have me for dinner."

Typical. Don comes for a beer, says his piece, and then leaves. What more can he ask for in a friend? "Fine. Rest assured I'll be making the call as soon as you leave."

"Good. I'm out." Don downs the rest of his beer and heads for the door. "Don't forget to call and let me know how it went."

"What are we, *besties* or something?"

Don laughs and lisps in his best female voice. "*Jessicaaa* to you, remember?" Then he strikes a pose.

Bo picks up another pillow and tosses it across the room. Don never misses a chance to make light of their childhood pranks. Jessica. Right. How can he forget that one? They had Bo's mom guessing for weeks who Jessica might be until she figured out they made her up just to get a rise out of her.

Don opens the door and turns to leave just in time for a man, dressed as a delivery person, to reach out and ring the doorbell. The man stops before he hits the button and looks at Don. "Sebastian MacLachlan?"

Don steps aside to let Bo step out onto the porch. "That's me."

The man hands Bo an envelope. "This is for you."

"What is it?"

"You've been served."

"Served? What do you mean *I've been served*?"

Bo looks at Don. Don looks back. They both look down at the brown letter-size envelope as the 'delivery man' snaps a photo of them and then turns and walks back down the driveway. Bo doesn't let him get far. "Hey!" He runs to catch up with him. "What is this? I didn't give you permission to take my photo."

The 'delivery man' reaches inside his pants pocket and pulls out what looks like a wallet. It flips down to show his identification card. "I work for a Process Server and the photo was to document personal service on you, Sebastian MacLachlan. You've been named as a Defendant in a lawsuit in the Common Pleas Court.

Bo looks at the identification card. The man in the picture is the man standing in front of him, but the rest is a blur. Who could be suing him? And for what? Bo heads back to his porch where Don is waiting.

Bo rips open the top of the envelope and pulls out a document. His name is shown as one of a long list of Defendants. "Complaint for Wrongful Death." Bo reads through the list of Defendants and finds himself. "Don, you and Greta are listed here too."

"What? Let me see." Don pulls the document from Bo's hands and flips through the pages.

"You should call Greta and let her know. Maybe it would be best to not be opening the door to anyone until we've talked to a lawyer."

Don starts walking to his jeep while he's tapping his phone with his thumbs. He waves back to Bo. "See ya, man. I gotta get home and see if Greta got this."

"Yeah, no problem. Let me know."

"And you need to call that girlfriend of yours and find out what's up."

"She's not my girlfriend."

Bo pulls out his phone and scrolls for her number as he closes the door behind him. He has no intention of considering Eva as his anything close to "girlfriend" now. That's for sure.

"I HAD NO IDEA THEY were going to *sue* you!" Eva's soft outburst draws attention to them.

Bo walks them to a corner of the gallery where he asked Eva to meet him. His artwork is being displayed and he thought it would be a good reason for them to meet up so he could talk with her. He didn't want to talk with her over the phone since she might decide to hang up and block him. And, he needs to know why she's doing this.

"Listen. My lawyer advised me not to speak with you. But, I need to know why, firsthand. From you. I thought we had..." Bo's voice cracks. "I mean..." Where is he going with this line of thought? Bo clears his throat. "What I mean to say is you gave me your number. I thought you wanted to get to know each other better. Not bring a lawsuit."

"And I thought you wanted to see me and share your first art gallery showing with me, which is phenomenal, by the way."

Bo chooses to ignore Eva's off topic side comment. "I did. I mean I do. But I need an explanation, Eva." He steps back to put some space between them. "This could ruin me. You must know that."

Eva rolls her lips and licks them. "To come straight to the point, if you look at the lawsuit or talk with your lawyer, the person suing is the *Estate*, not me."

"What exactly does that mean?"

"It's the lawyers for George's Estate. They wanted to bring the lawsuit. And let me tell you this. They are ruthless."

"Ruthless? Great." Bo runs his hand through his hair. "I'm ruined." He walks behind a wall into a closed off section to take a seat on a bench behind it. He needs privacy.

Eva follows him and sits next to him. Her company is welcome. She reaches over to take his hand in hers. "Please don't be mad at me. I swear to you I had nothing to do with this lawsuit. I didn't even know they filed one until you told me."

"It's your husband's Estate, Eva. You must have some say in the matter."

Eva pulls her hand away. "If you keep repeating my name to me, I might start requiring you to call me *Your Excellency*."

"What? What does that have to do with anything?"

"You want to start getting to know each other? Well, you can start by not beginning and ending your sentences with my name. George did that. It's condescending and I hate it."

Bo sits farther back on the bench and leans against the wall behind them. He takes a deep breath and closes his eyes to try and calm his nerves. Then he opens them again and glances over at Eva. This is not how Bo wanted their conversation to go. He's not sure how he expected it to go, but this is not it. Hurting Eva was not his intention even if he's the one at the receiving end at the moment. To see her distraught over something he initiated stabs him in his gut. This is not who he wants to be. This is not who he is. "So then, what do you suggest?"

Eva matches his position against the wall and looks over to him. "You need good lawyers."

Bo watches as she repositions that purple strand behind her ear. He restrains himself from reaching out to readjust it. Her brown, shoulder-length hair frames her face and accents her cheekbones causing a battle with his thought process. "Lawyers, as in plural?"

"Yes. A team of lawyers specializing in Estate Planning with experience in trial litigation is what you need."

Bo sits forward again. Wait a minute. He rubs his face with the palms of his hands. He glances back at Eva leaning against the wall. "Ev—hold up, hold up. I can't afford one lawyer, let alone a *team* of lawyers."

Eva's eyes stay on him. Bo can't help but question the color of her eyes. Weren't they blue when they first met? Now they look green. Why is he thinking about her eyes anyway? Eva doesn't remove her gaze from him. "I wish I could help you, but I can't. It would be considered a heavy conflict and if the media gets a hold of it, I'm sure you could imagine."

Bo turns to face forward and refocuses his attention to the conversation. The gravity of his situation further weighs in. "I don't know what could be worse than being accused of literally 'scaring' someone to death. Have you read the Complaint?"

Eva exhales through her teeth. "No. But I have an idea of their strategy."

Bo sits back against the wall again and turns to face Eva. "I stay away from news, in general. But there was no escaping this one. I limit myself to just the headlines when necessary, otherwise it would make me crazy, it's everywhere."

Eva reaches over to take his hand in hers. "I understand. I don't follow the media either. My staff keep me informed of what I may need to know and then they take care of the rest."

Bo's attention is drawn to her touch. Their hands mingle on the bench between them. "It must be nice." He exhales a deep breath and gently tightens their grip. He looks up and keeps his eyesight focused on what's in front of him— another white wall. No art. No meaning. Only two potted plants at each end. For greenery? Bo considers what piece of his artwork might make its debut in this space. Maybe its meaning is just that. Nothing. White emptiness. He can't tell if Eva is looking at him, but a warmth surges up his arm near where she sits. He wants to believe she's focused on him.

Bo can't fathom what might be waiting for him on the other side of this fiasco. Even spending time with Eva is a risk. Maybe he shouldn't have invited her to such a public place. The media hasn't caught wind of them. Yet. He needs to keep it that way. Does she really think his artwork is phenomenal?

EVA LOOKS OVER AT BO. His gaze is fixated on the white wall in front of them. His hand mingles with hers and feels safe and natural. The smell of his cologne. A spice scent? She leans her head against his shoulder. Will he flinch away? He doesn't. She settles a little closer. Safe and natural. A comfort similar to their first encounter starts to creep in. "Bo?"

"Yes?"

"Tell me what you're thinking?" Eva can tell Bo is struggling. There is nothing she can do. Or is there?

"It doesn't matter." Bo releases her hand and wraps his arm around her shoulders. Whatever happens, happens."

Eva's heart beats stronger. Her mind is racing. Her stomach flinches. "I want to make this— "

Bo catches her mid-sentence with his lips on hers. A sweet touch that sends her heart, mind, and stomach into a full-on fury of need. Eva reaches up to brush his cheek with her hand, just a tad, with the tips of her fingers. She can feel the slight jolt of his jawbone from her touch. His arms wrap around her midsection to pull her close against him. Eva relishes the warmth of his chest against hers. Even through clothes. Clothes she wishes were not between them. Bo cups her cheek with his hand sending her into a tailspin. His tongue meets with hers for the ultimate zing to her consciousness. Even more intense than the first time. Eva resists the urge to straddle him right then and there. But just barely. She's lost in the twirling of their hearts.

"Erm...excuse me, sir."

Just in time. Or not. Eva breaks the intensity of their lock to see who it is that entered the little haven they retreated to in the back of the gallery.

Bo moves a bit to the side. His face is flushed. "Yes, what is it?"

"I apologize for the intrusion, but some guests are interested in speaking with you about potential purchases asking where you are." This sharp-dressed gentleman looks at the floor. "I thought that might be of importance to you."

"Yes, yes, absolutely. I will be right there."

"Very well." The staffer bows his acknowledgment and turns to leave.

"Bo. I'm sorry." Eva doesn't know what else to say. Clearly, Bo needs to attend to his guests and here she is keeping him behind the scenes bungling about in his arms. What was she thinking? Eva fluffs up her hair a bit as if that would make any difference. She looks around for a mirror, but of course, there isn't one.

Bo stands up and offers his hand to her. She places it into his palm. Once more, zings and zangs starting from her midsection shoot through her body in all directions. This needs to stop. "Eva," Bo clears his throat. "I mean, *my lady*, there is nothing to be sorry about."

Eva smiles and lowers her eyes to the floor. She knows full well he's trying to accommodate her wishes by not starting and ending sentences with her name. She quite likes it. "I know you have to attend to your guests. And I just need to get this out there so, you know."

Bo places his hand on top of hers. Once more sending a less intense, although warm, vibe through her body. "What is it?"

"I didn't want to tell you like this. Especially, after... well, that."

Bo's hearty laugh only serves to make what she has to say harder.

"I need you to know I've enjoyed our time together immensely. I haven't felt like this in a long time."

"But?"

"But... I'm leaving to go home tomorrow."

"Tomorrow?" Bo's stance shifts. Eva can tell he's not pleased. His smile is gone again. "Will you be back?"

"I want to come back, but there are things back home that need my personal attention." Eva has no intention of telling him any more than that. Telling him she has to go home because her father insists is not something she likes to advertise. Telling him her parents were told of her little dalliance with him is not important. Telling him how she feels? Not yet and maybe never.

Bo stares down at her. His face is firm. His jaw clenches. "I understand. I hope you have a safe trip home." He drops his hands to his side. He leans in to give her a peck on the cheek and then turns to leave.

"Bo, wait."

Bo stops and turns to her. "Now who's starting their sentences with a name?"

Eva sighs. "Okay, well I needed you to stop and listen."

"And you thought I wouldn't understand unless you called my name?"

"Come on." Eva grabs his hand. "Please say we can stay in touch. Be friends."

Bo stares for a few seconds at their hands. "No. Long distance relationships never work."

"But how do you know until you try?"

"Believe me, I know. And just friends? I'm not interested. Life is too short."

Eva doesn't want to pressure him any further. It's clear he's had some kind of experience in the past. Besides, they've only known each other for a few weeks. She knew her time in the States was ending. Her heart begins to melt as she watches him walk back into the main gallery. Eva waits a few minutes before following him out. She takes a minute to enjoy Bo's talent by perusing through his paintings, taking in the composition, the shades of color that tug on the emotions of the observer. Imprinting his style on her brain.

Eva watches Bo's demeanor from a distance. She's never known anyone like him. Her heart sinks, the realization of what she has lost begins to bubble up again. How could she think that someone she only just met, whose arms she literally fell into, could be what she's been missing all her life? Someone who's been adversely affected by her, even if not directly? Someone who made it clear he doesn't want to be 'just friends.' Her breath gets caught in her throat when she thinks about that last thought. The answer is simple.

He can't be that person.

IREANNE CHAMBERS

CHAPTER FIVE

In the Fall, Cleveland and Medina, Ohio,
~ One Year Later ~

BO LEANS BACK ON HIS stool and folds his arms across his chest. He just unpacked his latest project assigned to him by The Cleveland Museum of Art. It's the newest addition to their medieval collection. His eye is immediately drawn to the raised paint along the edges. He can see the distinct brush strokes. Those should be easy enough to repair and replicate. The phone rings and Bo swivels around to reach for it on the desk behind him. "Hello?"

"Mr. MacLachlan, there is a gentlemen here by the name of *'Don'* who would like to speak with you."

"Sure, send him in."

"I'm not sure that's wise, sir."

Bo laughs under his breath. "It's fine. I know who he is. I've been expecting him. We'll steer clear of the paintings."

"Very well, sir."

Bo swivels back around and pulls out his cloth handkerchief from his pocket to wipe his forehead and his hands. He unfurls the corner to reveal his latest attempt to embroider his initials. He rubs his thumb across blue backstitched lines of "*SM*" when Don saunters in. "Time to go, broh."

Bo stands up, takes off his working coat, and hangs it up on the hook by the door. He picks up his newest Stetson Grey Bull from the next hook and strategically positions it on his head. "What do you think?"

Don flicks the rim of it once it's in place. Bo flinches backward to try and avoid it. "Dude, watch it. It's my latest addition. I'm trying to change it up."

Don *tsks* through his teeth and shakes his head. "I'll never understand you. I mean I know it's your look and all for when you're performing, but you don't have to wear them all the time. You're not in the country, in case you haven't noticed."

"How many times do I have to explain to you? I was raised all over the United States. I choose the country."

"Then why did you settle here?"

"I ask myself that same question." Bo knows the answer, but he has no intention of sharing. "Probably because it's where I went to high school. And then, you know the rest."

Don waits by the door while Bo removes his shoes and replaces them with boots. "Okay. You couldn't resist my company. I get it."

Bo stares at his friend. "You're crazy. Let's go." Bo shuts off the light and locks the door. "Tonight's show is sold out. I can't keep the fans waiting."

Don laughs. "Dude, I know you can sing. But, talk to me when you have a sold out stadium."

Bo flips his keys around in his forefinger while they walk to his truck. "You don't have to come if you don't want to."

"What? And miss all the line dancing?"

Bo unlocks the truck and gets in. "Venues like the Thirsty Cowboy are fine by me. I don't need sold out stadiums. It's more personal my way."

Don rolls down the window and bends his arm letting his elbow hang out. "Giddy up Cowboy, let's go!"

BO PULLS INTO THE THIRSTY Cowboy and pulls to the back where the VIP entrance is. A man comes out from a door next to a metal garage door wearing a black polo shirt and tan pants holding a clipboard at his side. Security. Bo rolls the window down. *Crunch, crack, crunch, crunch, crack.* The gravel of the parking lot reminds Bo of how the last year impacted him. It cracked him. It crunched him. It crunch-cracked and cracked-crunched him all the way to financial ruin. "Bo MacLachan. This is my assistant Don Gilbert."

The man pulls a pen from behind his ear, flips some pages on the clipboard, and writes on the page before placing the pen back behind his ear. "Right. Give me a minute. I'll go back and open the door and you can pull right into the backstage area."

"Thanks, man."

"You bet."

Bo waits for the door to roll up. He can tell Don is staring at him from his peripheral vision. "What? What is it?"

"Your assistant? Since when have I been your assistant?"

"Come on. I had to put you down as someone with me, otherwise you would have to pay for a ticket and no backstage entrance. Did you want me to call you my 'roadie'?"

Don pulls at the top of his baseball cap and slouches down in the seat. "Fine. But, don't make a habit of it. And, yes. Roadie would have been better."

EVA EXITS THROUGH THE sliding glass doors of Cleveland Hopkins Airport and a cacophony of bustling sounds immediately assault of her senses. The tang of exhaust fumes mixed with hot pretzels from a nearby vendor wafts towards her. She inhales deeply, a smile plays on her lips. Eva spots Naz waiting by a dark green Mercedes SUV, waving energetically. Naz's long, wavy hair sways with each enthusiastic wave.

"Naz!" Eva calls, her voice echoes slightly in the vast space. She rushes forward, dropping her carry-on to hug her friend tight.

"Eva, you're here! Finally!" Naz squeezes Eva with all her might. The familiar warmth of her friend's embrace makes Eva's heart swell.

The two pull back, and Eva takes in Naz's bright dark eyes and broad smile. "You look amazing, Naz. How is everything?"

Naz chuckles and picks up Eva's carry-on. "Busy as ever, you know lawyers. But I made time for you, didn't I? Tonight, I have a surprise. We're going to the Beck Center. There's a play, and you'll love it."

Eva raises an eyebrow. She's not sure if she will love it. Naz has always had a way with surprises and Eva isn't sure if she can handle another one. Last Fall's events have been plaguing her thoughts from the moment she decided to return for another season of cool Ohio weather and colorful foliage. Eva tries to match Naz's enthusiasm as they load the luggage into the trunk. "What's the play tonight?"

Naz winks playfully. "You'll find out soon enough."

Typical Naz.

The Beck Center buzzes with excitement. Eva's eyes roam over the crowd, a diverse mix of people. Freshly popped popcorn and the subtle hint of perfume create a familiar, comforting atmosphere. "I can't believe you managed to get tickets on such short notice."

Naz winks. "I have my ways. Besides, there's an art gallery attached. I thought you'd appreciate it."

Eva's heart skips a beat. She loves art, and Naz knows it. "You know me too well." Images of the last time she was at an art gallery force their way into her thoughts as they make their way to the gallery. Eva's eyes widen as she takes in the paintings on display. Vibrant colors, bold strokes, and an emotional depth that speaks directly to her soul. She stops in front of a series of paintings, her breath catches in her throat.

It can't be. Eva steps closer, her eyes scanning the signature. There isn't one, but she knows. The style, the texture, the depth of color, it's all there. Once more her mind races back to last Fall, the corn maze, the kiss. And Bo. The man she stumbled into. The man dressed as Count Dracula.

"Eva? Are you okay?" Naz's voice cuts through her thoughts.

Eva forces a smile, turning to face her friend. "Yeah, just... these paintings are incredible."

Naz is oblivious to Eva's inner turmoil. "Right? I heard the artist is anonymous. Adds to the mystery, don't you think?"

Eva swallows hard. "Yeah, definitely." She decides then and there that she must have these paintings. All of them.

"Let's find our seats." Naz tugs on Eva's arm in the direction of the theater while the lights dim and they settle into their plush seats.

The play does not disappoint. Only Naz would find a play adaptation from The Legend of Sleepy Hollow. Eva could not help laughing at the witty rendition with its entertaining dialogue and silly attempts to scare the audience. Yet still, Eva's mind keeps drifting back to the paintings. Bo's paintings. The way his eyes sparkled in the moonlight, the feel of his lips on hers. She shivers, the sensation is as vivid as if it happened yesterday. And then she remembers the day she left. How she left. Will he want to see her?

The final curtain call snaps Eva back to the present. Naz turns to her, eyes shining. "Wasn't that amazing?"

A genuine smile spreads across Eva's face. "It was perfect. Thanks for doing what you do best."

"What's that?"

"Coming up with the best ways to have fun and make unique memories, of course."

Naz gives Eva a squeeze around her shoulders as they exit the theater. Eva makes a beeline for the gallery. She finds the curator, a petite woman with glasses perched on the edge of her nose. "Excuse me." Eva's voice is steady. "I'd like to buy all the paintings by the anonymous artist."

The curator's eyes widen. "All of them?"

"Yes." Eva's voice is firm. "Absolutely sure. All of them."

Naz watches the exchange. A puzzled expression is on her face. "Eva, what's going on?"

Eva turns to her friend, a mixture of excitement and trepidation bubbles up. "I can't explain it right now, Naz. But trust me, this is important."

"Okay. You can tell me more over a cup of hot chocolate. I know a cozy café we can head to now."

Eva would rather head to Naz's condo. Tiredness from her trip across the ocean is beginning to set it. Or is it the fact that she's unsure about how Bo will receive her visit? She gives in. "Fine."

Silence takes over while Eva's lids begin to shut on the trip there. Naz finally breaks the silence. "So, are you going to tell me what that was all about?"

"Patience. Let's get the hot chocolate first, can we?"

At the café they settle into the closest seats by the fireplace. Eva's fingers trace the rim of her mug. Where should she start? "Remember last fall when I went to that corn maze?"

"Of course, I do. How could I forget about what happened to George."

Eva can feel a flush of warmth sneak through from her neck up to her cheeks. "And you remember Bo, right? He came to the hospital to check on us."

"Yes..."

"Well, we... had a moment. In the corn maze. In a Coffin. As Count Dracula." Eva rests her hand above her eyebrows. What must Naz think?

"Eva, I knew it! I had an inkling you two were up to something. Why didn't you tell me?"

Eva shakes her head and peaks at her friend. "I don't know. It didn't end very well. And those paintings? They're his. I just know it."

Naz's eyes widen. "You kissed a guy in a corn maze, dressed as Count Dracula, and now you're buying all his paintings?" Naz shakes her head side to side. "Eva, you have the best stories."

Eva laughs, a light, melodic sound that draws a few glances from nearby tables. "I guess I do. But there's something about his work. It's like he's speaking directly to me."

Naz reaches across the table and squeezes Eva's hand. "Maybe he is."

Eva looks out the window, the city lights twinkle like stars. She feels a sense of calm wash over her. Maybe.

COUNTESS WHO KISSED A COUNT

CHAPTER SIX

E va and Naz step into the Rock and Roll Hall of Fame. Crisp autumn air follows them inside through the arches of security, through the wall of glass doors, and to the desk to get their bracelet. The grand lobby is a sensory overload—bright colors from neon signs, a mini cooper hung from the ceiling, leather jackets and vinyl, and the sound of rock legends like Bon Jovi, Bruce Springsteen, and Journey echo through the halls. Eva breathes it all in enjoying the rush of excitement.

"This place is amazing." Naz's voice is a mix of awe and enthusiasm. She snaps pictures with her phone to capture every detail. "I've been here so many times with my membership and I still can't get enough.

"Yeah, it really is. And I'm sure they keep the exhibits updated." Eva tries to keep her nerves in check. She tugs at her scarf, feeling the soft wool against her neck, and glances around.

"Let's start with the main exhibit." Naz is already tugging at Eva's arm to move them toward the escalator to the lower level first so they can make their way up through the exhibits from there.

Eva falls in step beside her. They pass by glass cases displaying iconic memorabilia—Jimi Hendrix's guitar, a jacket worn by Elvis, handwritten lyrics by Bob Dylan. A phenomenal new Beatles exhibit. And Elvis! And Prince! Legends. Palpable blends of reverence and excitement radiates from the visitors. And some are moved to a spontaneous burst of song and dance. Strangers are instant friends bound by their love of music.

Just as they're about to turn a corner, Eva spots a familiar figure standing by a display of vintage concert posters. Eva's heart skips a beat. Bo. As handsome as ever, his blond hair tousled, and his eyes focused intently on the exhibit. For a moment, Eva considers ducking out of sight, but it's too late—he looks up and their eyes meet.

"Eva." Bo steps back, surprise is evident in his voice, although his facial expression quickly shifts to something more guarded.

"Bo." She tries to sound casual. "I didn't expect to see you here." Eva's not about to let on that she was looking forward to seeing him during this visit, while at the same time, not sure how to go about it.

Naz, ever the perceptive one, raises an eyebrow and then nudges Eva with a knowing grin. "I'll leave you two to catch up, I see a client over there who I'd like to pop over to and say hi. See you in a bit." Naz saunters off, leaving Eva and Bo alone.

The silence between them is thick and awkward. Eva fidgets with her scarf. Her focus is hovering over the rough texture of the wool under her fingers. She clears her throat. What can she say to break this silence?

"So...how have you been?" Eva cringes, the banality of the question.

Bo shrugs and slips his hands into his pockets. "I've been alright. Busy with work, you know."

"Right, are you still painting for that gallery?"

"Yes, among other things. And you? How's life treating you?" Bo's tone is neutral, but his eyes are searching.

"Busy as well." Eva tries to keep it light. Will he see through her awkwardness? "Naz has been dragging me to every possible event and exhibit. Today's the Rock Hall, tomorrow who knows?"

Bo chuckles. A shiver makes its way down Eva's spine. "That sounds like the life of a busy lawyer. Always on the move."

Another silence builds on the gap between them and the tension is almost tangible. Bruce Springsteen's Dancing in the Dark plays in the background and battles with the void for dominance. Chords tug at Eva's heartstrings. Chords that are too recognizable. "Look, Bo." Eva attempts to start, her voice is softer now, but she's still struggling to say what she prepared when their paths crossed. "About last Fall...I'm..."

Bo's expression hardens slightly. "No, really. We don't need to talk about it."

Eva bites her lip. A pang of guilt presses from the inside out. "Okay, we don't have to. I just— "

"—What?" His eyes lock onto hers. "Look, let's not. Let's let the past stay there." Bo sighs and runs a hand through his hair.

"Okay." Eva takes a step closer. "If that's what you want, Bo."

For a moment, Bo looks like he's about to say something more, but then he shakes his head. "Yeah, that's what I want. I think it's best. We can't change it."

Eva feels a mix of relief and sadness. "No, we can't. But maybe we can start over? As friends?"

Bo's lips twitch into a small smile. "Friends, huh? I guess."

Just then, Naz reappears, a mischievous grin on her face. "Hey, sorry to interrupt, but my client just left. Want to grab a coffee?"

Bo looks at Eva, a silent question in his eyes. "Sure, coffee sounds good."

As they walk towards the café, Eva suspects the fresh brewed coffee of a vintage kind is the house blend today. A table by the window opens up allowing the sunlight to cast its fall glow on their faces.

Bo orders his coffee, while Eva and Naz both opt for pumpkin spice flavored coffee. Eva's of course is milk, cinnamon, and a touch of coffee. The first sip is a burst of spices that warm Eva from the inside out.

"So, what have you two been up to?" Naz's eyes twinkle with curiosity.

"Just catching up." Bo glances at Eva. "It's been a while."

"Well, it's good to see you two talking. It's been too long."

Eva can't help but agree. As they chat and sip their drinks, awkwardness starts to fade, and is replaced by a version of camaraderie. Bo peeks at Eva creating a flicker of something. Could it be hope?

BO STANDS BEFORE THE massive canvas, his focus razor-sharp as he carefully applies the delicate brush strokes necessary to restore the painting's former glory. The familiar scent of linseed oil and old varnish fills the air, mingling with the faint aroma of fresh garlic and onions from the museum's gourmet restaurant and café. The Cleveland Museum of Art, quiet in the early morning, serves as a sanctuary for his thoughts. From the moment he hung up the phone with Eva, he has been questioning his reasons behind inviting her for lunch. Here. Where he works.

He's so engrossed in his thoughts and the canvas in front of him that Bo doesn't hear the soft footsteps approaching. A gentle clearing of the throat snaps him out of his reverie. He turns to find Eva standing a few feet away, her eyes sparkling with curiosity and amusement.

"Hey. I hope it's okay that I came to find you. One of the welcome people told me where to go." Her voice warms and teases. "I didn't know you were an art doctor."

Bo wipes his hands on a cloth and gives her a lopsided smile. "Art conservator, actually. But I suppose 'art doctor' works too."

Eva steps closer, her gaze wanders over the painting. "It's beautiful. You must have a lot of patience to do this."

"It's a labor of love." Bo can't help staring into her eyes. The familiar blue draws him in. And the familiar flutter of attraction stirs within him. He forces himself to stay grounded. "What would you like to do? Do you want to go for lunch now or after we do a tour?"

"I definitely want to check out the museum." Eva shrugs. "Maybe we can do that first?" A mischievous glint in her eye suggests otherwise.

Bo raises an eyebrow. Is she referring to what he thinks she is? Their last time together was also at an art gallery. Before she left him. Alone. With nothing. With nothing thanks to her husband's wrongful death lawsuit. He lost everything. "Good. Let's have lunch first."

Eva laughs and he remembers that sound. A sound he tried to elicit from her many times after her husband's death. Sometimes he was successful, sometimes not. "Okay, point taken. Let's eat first."

Bo feels a warmth spread through him, but he tries to keep his tone light. "Great. Let's head to the cafeteria. They have gourmet choices to choose from, no doubt you can tell from the spice."

"I love gourmet." Eva's eyes twinkle with excitement.

After lunch, Bo leads her through the gallery, pointing out different pieces and sharing little anecdotes about the artists. Eva listens, occasionally peppering him with questions that show just how keenly interested she is. The banter between them flows easily, a rhythm almost like before, but not quite.

As they reach a secluded corner of the gallery, Bo stops in front of a small, lesser-known painting. "This one's special." His voice is soft. "It's not the most famous piece here, but it has a lot of heart."

Eva tilts her head, studying the painting. "Why is it special to you?"

Bo hesitates. A sudden surge of vulnerability waffles through his insides. "It reminds me of us. Last year, before everything blew up. Fragile. New. Exciting."

Eva looks at him, her expression softens. "You're right. It was. It was all those things."

Bo turns to proceed down the hall. "We should go." His voice tight.

Eva touches his arm and steps closer. "I get that. Can we take a pause for a minute?"

Bo's heart races. The pull between them is undeniable, but he's wary of letting his guard down. "Eva, I can't. You don't know what it was like. Everything I had is gone."

Eva reaches out, her fingers brushing against his. The touch is electric, sending a shiver down his spine. "I'm so sorry. Sorry to have put you through that. I had no control over anything. It was the lawyers."

Before Bo can respond, the air between them crackles with tension. Eva leans in, her lips inches from his. The world around them fades away, leaving only the pounding of his heart and the intoxicating scent of her perfume.

Bo's resolve wavers. He knows he should hold back, keep his distance, but the temptation is too strong. Their lips meet in a hesitant kiss, the taste of wine from lunch lingers on her breath. Or maybe it's his. The kiss deepens, tongues tentatively explore, as if testing the waters.

Just as Bo loses himself in the moment, a loud voice startles them apart. "Well, well, well! What do we have here?"

Bo spins around to see Don grinning from ear to ear. "Don, this is...uh...Eva." Bo can feel his cheeks flush with embarrassment.

Eva, catches her breath and manages a smile. "Nice to meet you, Don."

Don raises an eyebrow, enjoying his catch of the day. "Nice to finally meet you too, Eva. I didn't mean to interrupt, but it looks like I walked in just in time." Don tugs on Bo's shoulders. "Can't have this guy losin' it, again."

Bo clears his throat, trying to regain his composure. "What? I didn't lose it. And, we were just talking."

"Sure, you were." Don winks at Eva. "Anyway, Bo, we have to leave for our meeting. Or, did you forget?"

"What meeting?" Bo gives Don a pointed look.

"So, you did forget. We were going to, you know. Meet up with Greta?"

Eva backs up a step and looks at Bo. "Greta?"

Don sniggers. "Greta's my wife." He saunters off and leaves Bo and Eva alone again. The interruption has shattered the moment, but the heat lingers between them.

Eva exhales, a mix of frustration and amusement. "Well, that was awkward. Do you have to leave?"

Bo laughs, the sound eases some of the tension. "Yeah, Don has impeccable timing. He means well."

Eva steps back into her closer position and rests her hand on his arm. "So, where do we go from here?"

Bo looks into her eyes, hope and uncertainty mirrors in his own. "I guess we take it one step at a time. No rush, no pressure."

"I can do that." Eva's soft breath teases him almost back to the testing waters. Almost.

As they walk back toward the main gallery, cautious optimism begins somewhere Bo's chest. The future is uncertain, but for the first time in a long while, he's willing to take a risk. Can this fragile, beautiful thing between them be restored?

COUNTESS WHO KISSED A COUNT

CHAPTER SEVEN

E va eases into the Thirsty Cowboy, taking in the rustic charm. Strings of twinkling lights crisscross the ceiling and cast a warm glow over the wooden interior. The air is thick with scents of pumpkin spice and fresh baked pies. The bar, adorned with autumn leaves and mini pumpkins, offers an inviting ambiance. Bo stands on stage, his Stetson hat tilted just right, guitar in hand, his voice like honey over gravel as he sings a soulful country ballad.

Eva makes her way to the front, her heart races as she catches Bo's eye. He winks, causing her cheeks to flush. She finds a spot at a high-top table near the stage and taps her fingers to the rhythm of the music. His voice fills the room, each note resonates in her chest, pulls her closer to him. The words sung, are sung to her.

When Bo finishes his set, the crowd erupts in applause. He steps down from the stage and makes his way toward Eva. She watches him, her pulse quickens. He moves with an easy grace, his eyes never leaving hers.

"Enjoying the show?" He slides into the seat next to her.

"You were amazing." Her voice is breathy. She tries to catch her breath without being obvious.

Bo's eyes sparkle with mischief. "Only amazing? I was going for legendary."

Eva laughs. The sound mingles with the country tunes playing in the background. "Alright, you were legendary. Happy?" Her breath is calmer, only just.

"Very" Bo leans in closer. His hand brushes against hers. A jolt of electricity maneuvers up her arm. "I got us something special to celebrate."

A waitress appears with two pumpkin spice cocktails. Eva takes a sip. The rich flavors of cinnamon and nutmeg dance on her tongue.

"This is delicious." Eva's eyes meet Bo's over the rim of her glass.

"Knew you'd like it." His voice low and intimate. Maybe even breathy. "Come on, let's dance."

Bo takes her hand and leads her to the dance floor. The music slows, and Bo pulls her close, his hand rests on the small of her back. Eva's heart pounds as they sway to the rhythm, the world around them fades away.

"You smell amazing." Bo's breath is mumbled and warm against her ear.

"It's the pumpkin spice." Eva jokes, though she knows he's not talking about the drink.

"No." Bo's voice is serious. "It's you."

Eva's breath catches in her throat. She looks up at Bo, their faces inches apart. His eyes are a deep, smoldering blue, darker around the iris. Their warmth makes her knees weak.

"You're pretty amazing yourself." Eva whispers while her hand slides up to rest against his chest while they move. She feels the steady beat of his heart beneath her palm. It matches the rhythm of her own.

Bo's thumb strokes her back in slow, soothing circles. "I've wanted to do this since the moment I saw you." Now his voice is husky.

"Kiss me?" Eva's lips curve into a teasing smile.

"That too," Bo leans in. His lips brush against hers, a soft, tentative caress that sends a shiver down her spine. The kiss deepens, their mouths move together in a slow, sensual dance.

Eva's fingers thread through Bo's hair, her body instinctively presses closer to his. She feels the heat of him, the strength of his arms around her, and she knows she's falling fast. Fast.

The sound of laughter breaks them apart. Don and Greta join them on the dance floor, Don's movements exaggerated and goofy as he tries to keep up with the music.

"Mind if we cut in?" Don winks at Bo.

"Be my guest." Bo steps back but keeps Eva's hand in his.

Don twirls Greta around, nearly knocking over a nearby couple. Eva laughs, the sound mingles with Bo's deep chuckle.

"Your friends are something else." Eva shakes her head.

"They're a handful." Bo's eyes twinkle. "But they're good people."

Eva watches Don and Greta, their antics bring a smile to her face. Don dips Greta low, only to stumble and nearly drop her. Greta swats at him, laughing as she does.

Bo pulls Eva back into his arms. "Let's show them how it's done." He spins her gracefully.

Eva's laughter bubbles up, pure and joyous. They move together, they step perfectly in sync. The music swells around them, a sweet, haunting melody fills the room.

Bo's hand tightens on her waist, his eyes never leave hers. "I'm really glad you're here, Eva." His soft voice envelopes her.

"Me too." Her voice barely a whisper.

They dance in comfortable silence, the world narrows down to just the two of them. Eva's senses are overwhelmed by him—the feel of his strong arms around her, the scent of his cologne mingling with the autumn air, the sound of his breath in her ear, the taste of his kiss lingering on her lips, the sight of his blond hair and handsome face so close to hers. Hiding them with his Stetson hat.

Don and Greta start a line dance, drawing more couples to the floor. Bo and Eva join in, their movements fluid and effortless. Don's exaggerated steps and Greta's playful swats keep everyone laughing.

"You two should take this act on the road," Bo calls out to Don, who responds with a grandiose bow.

"Only if you promise to be our opening act." Don winks at Eva.

Eva smiles, her heart swells with happiness. Bo's hand tightens around hers, a silent promise of more nights like this, more moments of laughter, more moments of love.

As the night winds down, Bo pulls Eva close once more, their bodies fitting together perfectly. "Thank you for tonight." His voice is now a low rumble.

"Thank you." Eva's eyes shine with emotion.

Bo leans in, his lips brushing against hers in a kiss that is sweet and tender, filled with the promise of a love that is just beginning. They stand there, wrapped in each other's arms, the music plays softly around them. Eva knows this must be the start of something wonderful.

BO WATCHES EVA'S EYES light up as she sips her pumpkin spice cocktail. It's almost closing time. The dim lighting of the Thirsty Cowboy casts a warm glow over her face. Her laughter mingles with the soft country music still playing in the background, Bo's heart swells with a mixture of affection and something deeper—something that feels different, new.

"Great set tonight," Don claps Bo on the shoulder. Greta stands beside him, her eyes sparkle with amusement.

"Thanks, Don." Bo's voice is casual. He looks back at Eva, who's engaged in conversation with Greta. "You ladies enjoying yourselves?"

"Yep." Greta grins. "Eva was just telling me about a painting she saw at the Beck Center."

Bo's smile falters. "Oh?"

Eva looks up, her eyes meet Bo's with a hesitant look. "Yes, the one with the barn and the sunset. It reminded me when I was here last fall."

Bo's chest tightens. "You've been to the Beck Center?"

Eva nods, a hint of nervousness in her expression. "Naz took me to see The Legend of Sleepy Hollow and there was an art display in the gallery."

Bo's eyes narrow. "Did *you* buy them?" Bo already knows the answer. He's not pleased.

Eva's face pales slightly, but she holds his gaze. "I—yes, I did."

Bo's heart drops. "All of them? The curator told me a young lady bought all of them— that was you?"

Eva nods again, her voice soft. "Yes. They are amazing renditions."

A storm brews inside Bo. "You bought them because of what happened last Fall, didn't you? Because of George?"

Eva's eyes widen, her voice trembles. "No, Bo. That's not it at all."

Bo's jaw tightens. "I don't need charity, Eva. I can take care of myself. The last thing I need is a woman to come and save me."

Eva's eyes fill with tears. "Bo, please. I knew you were the artist. I recognized your style, your brush stroke, your palette selection. I thought you would be pleased."

Bo steps back, the chair scraping against the floor. "Pleased? Those paintings were anonymous for a reason. They were a part of me I wasn't ready to fully share."

Eva's voice breaks. "I'm sorry. I didn't mean to hurt you."

Bo sighs, his anger mingles with frustration. "Eva, last Fall was a disaster. We got sued for all we had because George was '*scared to death*.' I don't need pity. I don't need help."

Eva's heart plummets. "Bo, please. You're misunderstanding my intentions. I bought them because they reminded me of happiness."

Bo's eyes soften, but the hurt remains. "Eva, you should have told me. I need honesty. No secrets."

Eva nods. Her voice is barely a whisper. "No more secrets."

Bo reaches out, his touch is both tender and firm. They stand there. The weight of emotion presses down on him. The lively atmosphere of the Thirsty Cowboy seems distant, overshadowed by the intensity of their connection. As the night draws to a close, Bo knows their journey is just beginning, though fraught with challenges. But, also filled with something else.

Eva wipes away a tear, her hand trembles. "I just wanted it to be like it was the last time we saw each other. Those paintings— when I saw them, they felt like pieces of you."

Bo's heart aches at the sincerity in Eva's eyes. "Eva, I need to know that you see me for who I am, not a man who needs saving. But, rather a man who can save."

Eva's voice trembles. "I see that man. A man who's passionate. Devoted. Charming and strong. I see you."

Bo pulls her into a tight embrace, his lips brush against her hair. "Eva..."

Eva wraps her arms around him. "Bo..."

They stand there, holding each other tight. Music plays softly around them. The Thirsty Cowboy's atmosphere begins to fade again as the night draws to a close.

IREANNE CHAMBERS

CHAPTER EIGHT

The sun sets over the rolling fields, casting a golden glow on the vibrant colors of autumn leaves. Bo's Chevy rumbles down the dirt path leading to the Corn Maze, its engine a comforting hum. Bo grips the wheel. Eva stares off in the distance. She's wearing a black velvet cloak, her dark, highlighted hair cascades over her shoulders with her purple lock, vivid and tucked behind her ear. The Fall evening is crisp, the scent of harvested corn and distant bonfires waft through the air.

"Remember the last time we came here?" Bo breaks the silence. "You tripped right into my coffin."

Eva's lips twitch into a smile. "How could I forget? You looked terrifying as Count Dracula. I still can't believe you managed to stay in character even when I fell on you."

Bo chuckles, the sound is deep and warm. "It's called dedication, my Countess. And who said anything about staying in character?"

"Well, as I remember it, you did take a little nibble of my neck." Eva's eyes glisten into their familiar twinkle.

"Ready to relive our eerie beginnings?" Bo winks continuing the enlightened the mood.

Eva allows herself to smile, just a little. The melancholy, well. Also, still there. "Yeah, let's go relive some memories."

They step out of the truck, the gravel crunches underfoot. The scent of popcorn and pumpkin spice fills the air. The laughter of children and the rustle of corn stalks create a festive atmosphere. Don and Greta are hanging out by the entrance. Greta has her makeup kit slung over her shoulder and waves enthusiastically. She's already dressed as a Princess Leah, her hair in equal buns on each side with dramatic black eyeliner.

"Look who's back for more!" Don calls out as he pulls Bo into a quick hug. He's in a simple scarecrow costume with straw that sticks out from his sleeves and pant legs.

"Can't get enough of this place," Bo replies as he claps Don on the back. "Where's Jimmy?"

"Probably lurking around somewhere with his costume rack," Greta pokes at her left bun. "He's got a new batch of costumes for us to try out tonight and probably some new scare tactics too."

As if on cue, Jimmy, a wiry man with his crooked grin, meets them at the entrance, wheeling a cart loaded with costumes. His face lights up when he sees Bo and Eva. "Well, if it isn't the Count! And his Countess, I presume?"

Eva chuckles, her mood begins to lift, a little. The sound of her voice is lighter now. "Nice to meet you, what do you have there for us?"

Jimmy grins pulling out a black cape with a red lining. "This should match your outfit perfectly. You're going to be the Countess to Bo's Count."

Eva takes the cape and runs her fingers over the fabric. A brief flicker of joy strikes down a pang of guilt. Does Jimmy know her background? Her true title?

Don nudges Bo. "You two ready for the big coffin scare again? We've got the same setup from last year."

Bo laughs. "As long as Eva doesn't trip into it again."

Eva playfully swats his arm. "Hey, that was a one-time thing."

Jimmy laughs while readjusting the costumes in his cart. "By the way, Bo, you've got to see this new setup. It's perfect for your YouTube video."

Bo sighs, Eva's stomach drops. Her disdain for social media sinks her mood just a bit. "Great, but I don't want to be too glued to my phone all night."

Eva brushes her hand against Bo's arm, a silent reassurance. "I'll try not to roll my eyes too much."

Greta jumps in, "I'm heading to the makeup tent. You guys coming? We can make you look even more undead."

"Sure, sounds fun." Eva inhales deep and makes an effort to smile and lift herself back up. Her emotions are running back and forth, up and down, like a game of tic-tac-toe.

They change into their costumes. Bo adjusts his cape, glancing at Eva as she emerges in a flowing black gown, her makeup pale and bright red lips.

"Wow, you look incredible." Bo's low and soft murmur serves to help Eva score on her emotional board of tic-tac-toe.

Eva's cheeks flush slightly. "Thanks, Bo. Ready to scare some people?"

They walk towards the maze, the crunch of leaves underfoot and the crisp air fills their lungs.

The sight of a child draped in a white sheet with eye holes cut out, muttering a dry "Boo" as they pass. Eva giggles, any lingering sadness is momentarily forgotten.

"Little Thing's back."

Bo calls out to the wandering sheet. "Hey, buddy. You scaring everyone tonight?"

The kid turns back solemnly. "Boo."

Bo chuckles and cups his hands around his mouth. "Keep at it, you're doing great!"

"Boo." Little thing repeats and continues his quest of wondering off into the maze.

As they walk further, they pass through a section of the maze decorated with hay bales and carved pumpkins. The air is filled with the sounds of laughter and faint creepy music playing in the background. The atmosphere is lively.

Eva links her arm into her Count's elbow. "So, Bo. What exactly is your name short for?"

Eva looks up at Bo, waiting for his response. He's conflicted. A few seconds pass. "Sebastian."

"Wow! I would not have guessed that."

Bo smirks and pats Eva's hand where it rests. "They had high hopes for me. Thought I'd be an artist like Bach. Sent me to music and art school."

"And now you're a famous YouTuber with thousands of subscribers," Eva teases. "Guess you didn't disappoint."

"Yeah, well, I doubt they expected me to be painting corn mazes and making horror skits." Bo shakes his head.

They reach the center of the maze where the coffin setup waits. The sight brings back memories of their first meeting where Eva tripped and fell right into the coffin where Dracula had been hiding. It was embarrassing, endearing and— Eva's thoughts took her through to the culmination of that evening— George.

"Perfect timing." Greta's announcement brings her Eva back to now.

A light flush of warmth tickles Eva's cheeks. "Thanks."

Bo taps Eva's hand again. "Ready for another round in the coffin?"

Eva takes a deep breath before they climb into the coffin together, squeezing into the tight space. It's dark, and the scent of old wood and makeup fills the air. Eva can feel Bo's warmth beside her, and the intimacy of the moment stirs something deep within.

"This is ridiculous," Eva whispers, but she can't help enjoying the whimsical flips and zing-worthy antics shooting throughout her body.

"Maybe," Bo murmurs back. "But it's our kind of ridiculous."

Greta closes the coffin lid, plunging them into darkness. Eva can hear the muffled sounds of people navigating the maze, their footsteps drawing nearer. Bo's hand finds Eva's and their fingers intertwine.

"Do you think they'll scream as loud as last year?" Eva's voice is barely audible.

"Only one way to find out." Bo creaks open the coffin lid and they sit up, fangs fluorescent and greenish-white. A group of teenagers shriek and stumble back with complete terror. Bo and Eva burst out laughing, the shared moment eases any tension Eva had up until now. Bo closes them back into the coffin for the next victim.

"I'm sorry, Bo," Eva's soft whisper trembles as she speaks. "I didn't mean to hurt you. I just wanted to support you."

"What?" Bo shuffles to the side so he's facing her.

Eva blurted it out. Not the best choice in timing, but she needed him to know. "The artwork. I'm talking about the artwork. I need to tell you. I'm sorry."

Bo squeezes her hand. "I know, Eva. I overreacted. I was just shocked. But I think I understand why you did it."

Eva looks to the side to hide the tears welling up. "I never wanted to betray your trust. I love your work and believe in you."

Bo reaches over and untangles a strip of her hair. "And I love you, Eva. I should've seen it as the act of love it was."

Eva shuffles to face him. "You do? Really?"

"Yes, really." Bo cups her face with his one free hand, leans close, and meets her lips in a tender kiss.

The coffin is less cramped. The darkness, less suffocating. Eva pulls back and gazes into Bo's eyes, past tensions dissolve into nothing. "I love you too."

Bo pulls her back to him and readjusts his arms so that he's holding her. And kissing her. And caressing her cheek with the back of his hand. And kissing her. Eva mingles her tongue with his craving the zings. Electric, warm, inviting zings and zangs. All the sounds around them fade into nothing. Nothing else is more important than Bo. And what he was doing to her now, in this moment. A moment Eva doesn't want to stop.

The coffin lid is yanked open and Don's face appears. "You lovebirds done in there?"

Bo and Eva climb out, laughing. "Is it over already?"

They join Don and Greta, heading back to the main area. More scares progress along the way. They end up with Don and Greta near the food stalls. Scents of hot cider and caramel apples mingle with the chill of the night air.

"Eva, did you know Bo's a vegetarian?" Greta bites off a piece of her spiced jerky.

Eva looks at Bo. "I did know that."

Bo sips his boilermaker. "Yep. And I know you're a serious carnivore."

"Guess we balance each other out." Eva pulls at her own spiced jerky.

Greta looks at Don, "Yeah, it's good when you can balance each other."

Greta and Don say their goodnight's and Bo and Eva make their way back to Bo's truck. Bo pulls out his phone, setting up a camera for a quick YouTube video.

"Hey, guys! Bo here with my Countess, Eva. We're at the Corn Maze where it all began. Hope you're all enjoying the fall season!"

He signs off, turning to Eva. "You okay with that?"

Eva and social media do not go well together. But still, it's a small compromise. She smiles and cuddles close to Bo. "As long as I'm with you."

Bo pulls a blanket from the back seat and lines the bed of his truck. He holds out his hand to help her in. Eva steps up and Bo follows. Eva settles into his arms as they lie back and stare up at the clear midnight sky, scattered with stars. Bo wraps his arm around Eva and snuggles close. The frosty night air brushes against their skin, but the warmth between them keeps the chill from sinking in.

"Look at that." Bo points to the clear sky. "That's Orion, the hunter."

Eva nestles closer into his side, her head rests on his shoulder. "It's beautiful."

"Just like you." Bo's breath is warm against her cheek.

Comfortable contentment settles in. The world around them fades away, and Eva is lost in the vast expanse of the night sky and warmed by the man beside her. The sounds of the maze, the laughter, the screams, drift in the distance.

Eva slips her hand into Bo's, their fingers intertwine. "I'm glad we came back here."

"Me too." Bo whispers as he presses a kiss to her forehead. "Me too."

Under the blanket of stars, Eva's thoughts wonder. Is the past the past? Can the future really be wide open? Like the endless sky above?

COUNTESS WHO KISSED A COUNT

CHAPTER NINE

B o and Don exit the Thirsty Cowboy, the sound of twangy guitar riffs and rowdy applause still echo in Bo's ears. The night air hits his face, a stark contrast to the stuffy warmth of the bar. Bo's heart races with the adrenaline of his performance, but also a nagging exhaustion pulls at him.

"Great set tonight, Bo," Don claps him on the back. "You really had the crowd going."

"Thanks, Don. Means a lot coming from you" Bo fishes his keys out of his pocket.

They climb into Bo's maroon Chevy. The leather seats creak under their weight. The engine rumbles to life, and Bo steers them onto the dark country road. The night is still. The only sounds are the hum of the truck and the distant chirping of crickets.

"Man, I could use a burger right now." Don stretches out in his seat.

"I know a place that's still open. They make a mean veggie burger." Bo grins at his co-pilot sitting next to him and waits for what he knows is coming.

Don scoffs. "Veggie burger? You know I don't eat grass burgers."

"Just trust me, alright?"

The truck's headlights cut through the darkness, illuminating the winding road ahead. Bo laughs with Don while he's explaining his latest failed attempt at fishing when the headlights suddenly catch a pair of swerving lights ahead.

"Bo, watch out!"

A sickening crunch of metal on metal. A blinding flash. And darkness.

Pain radiates through Bo's body. Consciousness fades in and out with blurs of flashing lights and distant voices. Each breath is a struggle. His body jostles side to side. They must be lifting him. The whir of helicopter blades fill his ears. Someone's shouting, but the words are lost in the haze.

Bo wakes again in a sterile room. Sharp antiseptic invades his nostrils. Beeping monitors are relentless, grounding him in this new reality. Don's face swims into view with a mix of relief and worry etched into his features.

"Don." Bo voice croaks in his throat, dry and scratchy.

"Hey, *broh*, you're awake." Don's voice is thick with emotion. "You're at the Cleveland Clinic. They life-flighted you here."

Bo's mind struggles to piece together fragments of memory. "What happened?"

"We were hit by a drunk driver. You took the brunt of it. I... I'm so sorry, Bo," Don's voice breaks.

Bo's chest tightens, the weight of reality settles in. "Are you okay?"

"Just some minor injuries. Nothing compared to you." Don's eyes glisten with tears.

A doctor enters the room with a clipboard in hand. "Mr. MacLachlan, Sebastian? I'm Dr. Richards, your neurosurgeon. We need to discuss your condition."

"Bo. Just call me Bo." Bo braces himself, dread pools in his stomach. "What's the verdict?"

Dr. Richards takes a deep breath. "You've sustained severe spinal injuries. As it stands, you're paralyzed from the waist down. There's a possibility that surgery could help you regain some mobility, but it's risky."

"What kind of risks?" Bo's voice is barely above a whisper.

"There's a chance the surgery could worsen your condition, potentially leaving you paralyzed from the neck down." Dr. Richards' tone is somber.

Bo's mind reels, the weight of a decision this monumental crushes him. "And if I don't do the surgery?"

"You'll remain paralyzed from the waist down. But you'll avoid the risk of further injury. You don't have to make a decision now. We can discuss this more after you've recovered from the initial trauma." Dr. Richards' tone doesn't falter.

"Thanks, Doc. I need some time to think." Bo's voice is now hollow.

Dr. Richards leaves the room nodding with a sympathetic glance. Don sits beside Bo, a steady presence of comfort.

"What do I tell my parents, Don? They always had such high hopes for me. And what about Eva?" Bo's voice begins its cracking. Eva.

"You don't have to tell them anything right now if you don't want to." Don tightens his lips and rolls them inward. "I'll support whatever you decide."

"I don't want them to know. They'll blame themselves for pushing me so hard. They wanted me to be an artist, but this... this isn't what they imagined," Tears stream down Bo's face.

Don squeezes his shoulder. "Alright, we won't tell them. But you're not facing this alone, Bo."

Greta enters the room, her face is a mask of concern. "Hey, Bo. How are you holding up?"

Bo forces a smile. "I've been better."

"We were talking, and we think setting up a GoFundMe could help with the surgery costs. You don't have to decide anything now, but I wanted you to know we got you." Greta's gentle voice is soothing.

"No. No." Bo shakes his head from side to side. "I don't want pity or charity. You know this about me." Bo snaps at his friends. His frustration is bubbling over.

Don's voice is firm. "It's not pity, Bo. People care about you. They want to help,"

Bo shakes his head again more profound. The thought of being a charity case is too much to bear. "I can't. I won't."

"Just think about it, okay? Like I said, you don't have to decide right now," Greta's eyes are pleading with him.

Bo closes his eyes, the weight of the world pressing down on him. Eva's gentle, beautiful face with her purple strand of hair dangling on one side appears on the inside of his eyelids surrounded by a blood-mahogany backdrop. "No, I don't want the surgery. I can't take that risk."

"Bo, please. Don't decide now. Just consider it." Bo can hear Don's voice breaking like his own was. "You deserve a chance to get better."

Bo opens his eyes, meeting Don's earnest gaze. He stares at his good friend since high school. Moments pass. "Fine. I'll think about it. No promises."

Greta squeezes Bo's hand. Her touch is warm and reassuring. "Good. That's good."

As they sit in silence, the gravity of Bo's situation hangs heavy in the air. Decision looms before him. A path fraught with uncertainty and fear. Maybe he should get in touch with his parents. He'll do that later.

Under the harsh hospital lights, Bo's thoughts hang onto Eva. Bo makes a silent vow— to himself. Whatever happens, this will not define him. He'll find a way to keep going, no matter how difficult the road ahead may be.

EVA'S FINGERS TIGHTEN around her phone as she stares at the text from Naz: "Urgent. Call me ASAP." She dials instantly. Her heart races as she paces Naz's condo. She knows it must be bad for Naz to stop in the middle of her day dealing with her clients and their immigration issues.

Naz's voice crackles through the line. "Eva, it's about Bo."

Eva's breath catches. "What happened?"

"Bo and Don were in a serious accident last night." Naz's voice is steady yet filled with underlying tension. "A drunk driver hit them head-on after they left the Thirsty Cowboy."

Eva's legs buckle and she collapses onto her bed. "Is he...?"

"Bo's paralyzed from the waist down. He's at the Cleveland Clinic." Naz voice is softer now.

Eva's mind spins. Naz's words sinking in like a cement block thrown in the mud. She forces herself to speak. "I need to get there. Can you take me?"

"Of course. I'll pick you up in ten."

The ride to the Clinic is surreal. The streets of downtown Cleveland a blur outside the car window. The familiar scent of leather in Naz's Mercedes and the distant hum of city traffic are disconnected from the gravity of this news.

Eva's voice trembles. "How is he handling it?"

Naz glances at her with dark eyes filled with concern. "Bo's refusing to let Don and Greta set up a GoFund Me page for starters. He doesn't want charity."

Eva shakes her head, tears threaten to spill. "That's so typical of him. Always the strong one, never asking for help."

"He's being stubborn, in my view." Naz's grip on the steering wheel tightens. "From what you've told me about him so far, Bo's always been the provider, the one who helps others. He hates being on the receiving end."

Eva swallows hard. Her mind races with memories of Bo. His laughter, his strength. "Why can't he see that he deserves help too?"

Naz sighs with heavy empathy. "I don't know. I think it's hard for men, in general. Accepting help means accepting that he needs it."

The silence between them grows thick. Unspoken fears and hopes fill the space. Blooming flowers from a passing market briefly waft through the car. Life's fleeting beauty. What an ironic reminder.

Eva's voice is barely audible. "I can't stand the thought of him suffering, Naz. He's so full of life. His music. His artwork. His stupid hat."

Naz reaches out and gives Eva's hand a reassuring squeeze. "We'll figure out a way to help him, Eva. He needs all the support he can get right now, even if he doesn't realize it. And he can still sing and paint."

As they pull into the Clinic's parking garage, the imposing building looms ahead, stark, sterile and white. Eva's stomach churns, the gravity of the situation hits her anew.

Naz parks and turns to Eva. "Are you ready?"

Eva nods, though her heart feels anything but ready. "I have to be."

They walk into the Clinic, the antiseptic mingles with the faint aromas of hospital food. Bright fluorescent lights reflect off the polished floors, casting a harsh glare that makes Eva squint.

Naz leads the way to the elevator, and they ascend in tense silence. The soft ding as they reach the fourth floor feels like a death knell. Eva's heart pounds in her chest.

Naz stops outside Bo's room. "I'll wait here, give you two some privacy."

Eva is grateful for her friend's understanding. She takes a deep breath and steps inside. The sight of Bo lying in the hospital bed, pale and vulnerable, brings fresh tears to her eyes.

"Bo," her voice breaks between her whispers.

Bo's eyes open and a faint smile follows. "Eva... you came."

She rushes to his side, taking his hand in hers. The feel of his cool skin against her warm fingers sends a jolt through her. "Of course I did. I'm so sorry, Bo."

Bo squeezes her hand. His grip is weak. "It's not your fault. It's just... life. Unforeseen occurrences."

Eva shakes her head. Her tears stream down her cheeks. "We'll get through this. Together."

He gives her a sad smile. "I don't want pity, Eva. Or charity. I can't stand the thought of being a burden."

"You're not a burden." Eva's voice is fierce. "You've always been there for people. Let us be there for you now."

Bo closes his eyes, a single tear slips down his cheek. "I don't know if I can."

Eva leans down and presses a kiss to his forehead. "You don't have to do this alone. We'll figure it out, I promise."

Naz's gentle knock on the door interrupts them. "Eva, we should let Bo rest."

Eva gives Bo's hand one last squeeze. "I'll be back soon, okay?"

Bo's eyes remain closed, but he nods. "Okay."

Eva steps out into the hallway and the weight of the moment presses down on her. She feels Naz's comforting presence beside her like a steady constant in the twisting of her emotions.

They walk back to the car in silence. The reality of Bo's situation hangs heavy in the air. Eva knows the road ahead will be difficult, but with Naz's support and her love for Bo, she will find a way. She'll pay for the surgery herself.

BO SITS IN HIS LIVING room. Light filters through the sheer curtains casting a soft glow on the wooden floors. A faint smell of incense, a remnant of his parents' influence, mixes with the rich aroma of fresh coffee. The room is stifling. A prison. A prison of his own making. His wheelchair creaks when he shifts, the sound grates against his nerves.

A knock on the door startles him. Before he can react, his mom, Rose, opens the door. Always the free spirit. Always with long silver hair and a tie-dye dress of some color of the day.

"Bo, you have a visitor." Rose's singsong voice resonates against the walls.

Eva steps in, her eyes immediately find his. Her presence dominates and a wave of emotions wash over him. A mix of relief and dread overcomes him.

"Eva, what are you doing here?" Bo's voice is harsher than he intended.

Eva doesn't flinch. "You've been avoiding me. I had to see you."

Bo's dad, Hank, ambles in carrying a tray of herbal tea. Bo watches his Dad with his gray beard and kind eyes. He always felt nothing but kindness from his hippie Dad. And his hippie Mom, for that matter. His Dad's age is showing more this visit. Earthy scents blend in with the incense, creating a calming ambiance. Bo finds it anything but soothing no matter how kind the intention.

"Hello, Eva. Nice to see you," Hank sets the tray down on the coffee table.

Eva smiles politely. "Hi."

Bo's frustration bubbles over. "Stop acting like you know each other. Mom, this Eva. Dad, this is Eva. Eva, these are my parents." Bo wheels himself around to face the coffee table and knocks into the side table. More frustration sends him reeling.

"I can't navigate my own house. How do you expect me to live like this?"

Rose's eyes soften. "We're here to help you, Bo. All of us."

Bo continues his struggle to maneuver his wheelchair, but the edge catching on the rug. Bo's anger rises, a hot glow builds from his chin to his forehead. "I don't want your help. I don't want anyone's help."

Eva steps forward, her voice is steady. "Bo, please. Let us support you. You don't have to go through this alone."

Bo's mom nods in agreement. "She's right, honey. And surgery could change everything."

Bo shakes his head. Now, the pressure building in his chest adds to the red-hot of his face. "No. I refuse to be a charity case."

Hank places a gentle hand on Rose's shoulder. "It's Bo's decision, love."

Rose's eyes well up with tears. "But he needs this."

Eva stands up to kneel next to Bo. "And, I want to help. Please let me help. Let me pay for the surgery. I have the means. Please."

Bo's anger cracks into his voice. "I need you all to stop treating me like I'm helpless." He tries to maneuver his way around and out of the room.

Eva's eyes fill with tears. "We don't see you that way, Bo. We care about you. I care about you."

A pang stabs in his heart. He doesn't want to push her away. But he can't bear the thought of being a burden. "Eva." Bo stops trying to fiddle with the wheel and looks at Eva positioned at his level. "I appreciate it, but I need you to go."

Eva's face falls. Pain in her eyes mirror his own. She slowly rises up and her voice is barely above a whisper. "If that's what you want."

Bo's heart aches. He watches her as she turns to leave. "It's not about what I want. It's about what I need."

Eva pauses at the door, looking back one last time. "I'll be here if you change your mind."

The door closes behind her. Silence in the room is oppressive. Bo's parents exchange a look of concern between them.

Rose breaks the wall. "You're pushing away the people who love you, Bo."

Bo's is almost riotous. "I can't let them see me like this."

Hank's voice is gentle and firm. "You're stronger than you think, son."

Bo's eyes burn. Unshed tears begin to flow down his cheek. "I don't know how to do this."

Rose kneels beside him. She takes his hand in hers in a way only a mother can. "One step at a time, honey. One step at a time."

Bo's resolve weakens and the weight of pride and fear presses down on him. He knows his parents are right, but accepting help, it's like admitting defeat. And he will not be defeated. He sits there surrounded by the warmth of his parents' love. Maybe he doesn't have to face this alone.

IREANNE CHAMBERS

CHAPTER TEN

E va spots Bo under the old oak tree in the park, the one with the sprawling branches that cast dappled shadows on the ground. He sits in his wheelchair, his hands clenched on the armrests, his face a mask of irritation. It's been weeks since she last saw him, and the distance has only sharpened her resolve. Rose and Hank chat nearby with voices low and conspiratorial. Eva takes a deep breath, and heads in Bo's direction.

Rose waves Eva over. A hopeful smile spreads across her lips. "Eva, dear, so glad you could make it."

Bo's eyes narrow. "Mom, what is this? Why is she here?"

Hank steps forward with his gentle demeanor, a stark contrast to Bo's simmering anger. "We thought it might be good for you two to talk."

Eva approaches, her heart is aching at the sight of Bo's frustration. "Bo, please. Just hear me out."

Bo's gaze locks onto hers, his dark blue eyes are almost black from unspoken pain. "I'm not changing my mind."

Eva's voice softens and she takes a seat on a bench next to him. "I'm here because I care about you. I've missed you."

"Eva," Bo's voice is edged with irritation. "I didn't expect to see you here."

"I thought it was time we talked."

Bo's gaze shifts to his parents. "So this was your doing?"

Rose's sheepish smile slowly spreads across her face. "We thought it might be good for you to see her."

Bo's jaw tightens, but he turns back to Eva. "Fine. Let's talk."

Eva sits on the bench beside him, the distance between them feels like a chasm. She takes a deep, earnest breath. "Bo, I know things have been hard. And like I said I've missed you and I have something important to tell you."

Bo snorts and looks away. "Well, get on with it."

Eva's voice trembles. She swipes the palm of her hands in unison down her thighs on the front of her pants. "Yes, okay. Let me explain. I just need to say it. My parents are Royalty in Thalassia, a small country on the Mediterranean coast. That's in addition to the Countess title I inherited when I married George."

Bo's head snaps at her, anger flares in his eyes. "We agreed. No more secrets."

Eva's eyes well with tears. "I know, and I'm sorry. I thought it wouldn't matter, but it does. Especially now."

Bo's fists clench on the armrests of his wheelchair. "So what now? Another secret?"

Eva shakes her head, determination hardens her gaze. "No. I'm offering you a job. Come to Thalassia and paint portraits of my family."

Bo's face is a layer of frustration mixed with betrayal. "You think a job offer makes this better?"

Rose steps in, gentle yet firm. "Bo, listen to her. This could be a good opportunity."

Hank places a hand on Bo's shoulder. "Change of scenery might do you some good, son. You're a talented artist."

Bo looks at his parents. Eva follows his line of sight. Their concern and love are clear in their eyes. Bo shifts his gaze back to Eva. "Why now? Why this?"

"Because I believe in you. Because I love you. Because I've seen your talent. And your passion. This isn't just about the job. It's about giving you a chance to do what you love."

"I can't even navigate my own house without help. How do you expect me to travel and work?"

Eva's eyes shine with determination. "My family has resources. We can make it work."

Rose kneels beside him. "Bo, please. You've always been strong. Don't let this defeat you."

Hank chimes in steady and reassuring. "You're not alone in this. We're here, and so is Eva."

"And what if I fail?"

Eva reaches out to touch his hand. Her unwavering faith in him shines like lighthouse for his dark thoughts. "Then we try again. Together."

Eva watches as Bo closes his eyes. The weight of their words hopefully sinking in. The scent of the park, the sound of children laughing and playing in the leaves off in the distance. If only she could take his pain away. Help him feel grounding and safe. Remind him his life is still full of possibilities.

Rose's voice breaks the silence. "You've always been talented, Bo. Don't let this accident take that away from you."

Bo opens his eyes, meeting his mother's gaze.

Eva's voice is filled with conviction hoping to drive him forward with her words of truth, love, and belief in him. "Come to Thalassia, Bo. Let's see what we can create together."

Bo looks at his parents, then back at Eva. The decision looms large, but for the first time in weeks, he feels a glimmer of hope. "Alright," he says, his voice steady. "I'll consider it."

Eva's face lights up with relief, and Rose claps her hands together. "That's my boy."

Hank smiles, squeezing Bo's shoulder. "You won't regret this, son."

Bo takes a deep breath and hesitates. The path ahead is still uncertain but no longer insurmountable. The future, once bleak and daunting, now holds a flicker of promise. Eva stands, offering her hand to Bo. "Let's take it one by one."

In the Fall, City of Tripolia, Country of Thalassia
BO'S EYES WIDEN AS he takes in the opulence of the palace grounds. Marble columns line the expansive courtyard, lush gardens overflow with vibrant blooms, and the Mediterranean Sea shimmers in the distance, casting a golden hue in the late afternoon sun. Saltwater and the sweet aroma of jasmine are carried by the gentle breeze. So, this is Fall on the other side of the world.

Eva pushes his wheelchair across the cobblestone path, her voice is cheerful. "You'll love my parents. They're very welcoming."

Bo's stomach knots into a mix of nerves and irritation. "Welcoming, huh? Like how you welcomed me with another secret?"

Eva's smile falters. "Bo, I—"

Before she can finish, the grand doors of the palace swing open, revealing King Timotheos and Queen Rena. Timos, as

Eva called him, stands tall in regal attire. He must be six feet or taller. His presence commands attention. Rena is elegant and poised while she descends the steps with a warm smile.

"Eva, darling, you're home!" Rena's voice is melodic. A hint of an accent adds to her charm.

Eva tightens her grip on Bo's wheelchair. "Mother, Father, this is Bo."

Timos steps forward, his eyes sharp, but kind. "Welcome, Bo. It's an honor to meet you."

Bo clears his throat, and a bit out of place. "Thank you, Your Majesty."

Rena laughs lightly. "Please, call us Timos and Rena."

Bo nods his head almost like a bow and his discomfort remains. "Right. Timos and Rena."

They lead Bo and Eva into a grand hall, where ornate tapestries hang from the walls, and chandeliers sparkle above. Polished marble floors reflect the grandeur of the room. Freshly polished wood and a hint of lavender accentuates the air.

Servants bustle about offering Eva first, and then Bo a glass of chilled wine. The crisp taste serves as a refreshing element on his palate. He watches Eva move with ease in this world of luxury. The gap between them begins to widen.

Eva glances at Bo with a hopeful expression. "Bo, this is where I grew up. It's a bit much, I know."

Bo takes another sip of wine, his irritation is flaring. "A bit much? Eva, I knew you were a Countess. Now I find out you're a Princess too?"

Eva exhales a sigh. "In practice, it's not much different."

Humorless, Bo laughs. "Not much different? Look around, Eva. This is a whole other world."

Timos and Rena approach them exchanging looks of question and concern. Rena steps forward, her voice is gentle. "Eva has always valued simplicity despite our status. She wanted you to know her for who she is, not her title."

Bo shakes his head with frustration evident. "It's not just about the title. It's about trust. We agreed, no more secrets." Why does he have the intense desire to explain himself?

Eva kneels beside his wheelchair, both her hands rest on his, one on top of the other. "I'm sorry, Bo. I didn't mean to hurt you. I just didn't think it mattered."

Timos clears his throat in an obvious change of subject. "Bo, Eva tells us you're a talented artist. We'd love to see your work."

Bo glances at Timos, the sincerity in his words is there, but Bo still struggles with the situation. "I appreciate that."

Eva stands. A flicker of relief crosses her face. "Bo's work is incredible. It's why I want him to be the artist chosen to paint this year's family portraits."

Rena's warm smile reappears as if on cue. "That sounds wonderful, darling."

Bo's tension eases only slightly, but he remains wary. "Thank you. I'd like that."

A different servant enters the room and announces dinner. The group moves to the dining hall, where a feast awaits. The rich aroma of the country's herbs and spices frolic in the air. Bo's mouth waters. They settle at the long, polished table. Vegetarian options are offered along with the roasted lamb.

Sounds of silverware clink along with soft conversation creating a surprisingly intimate atmosphere.

Bo observes the cultural nuances—Timos and Rena's graceful gestures, the Mediterranean dishes that are both exotic and inviting. He feels a twinge of discomfort in the revelation of how different his own family's dinners are back home. The differences in how they were raised, the differences in countenance— hippies and royalty?

Midway through the meal, Timos leans forward, curiosity is evident his eyes. "Bo, tell us about your family."

Bo hesitates, his thoughts turning to his modest upbringing. His hippie parents. "My parents are great. Not royalty, but they're the best people I know."

Rena's smile is genuine. "We'd love to meet them someday."

Bo forces a smile. The disparity between their worlds looms large. "Maybe someday."

After dinner, as they walk through the gardens, the sun sets over the sea. A warm glow casts its presence on everything. Bo looks at Eva and her face is immediately lit by the golden light. His heart aches with love. And frustration.

"Eva, I don't know if I fit into this world of yours." Bo's voice is raw. He doesn't mean it the way it sounds. But it's raw.

Eva's eyes well up with tears. "Bo, it's not about fitting in. It's about us, about what we can be together."

Bo's mind races with doubts and fears and then doubts again. "Your world is so different from mine."

"We can face those challenges."

Bo looks into Eva's amber eyes, uncovered in blue contacts. Her matter-of-fact response with sincerity and desperation undoes him. He wants to believe her, but the gap between their worlds is insurmountable. Love might not be enough to bridge the divide. For now, he decides to take it as they agreed. One by one. "We'll see, Eva. We'll see."

COUNTESS WHO KISSED A COUNT

CHAPTER ELEVEN

B o adjusts his Stetson hat, the brim casts a shadow over his eyes. The warm, Mediterranean breeze rustles the leaves of the olive trees surrounding the palace courtyard where he has set up his easel. Eva watches as he adjusts it lower to match closer to the level of his wheelchair. She remembers when she first saw him working on canvas at the Art Museum back in Cleveland. He was sitting on a stool with a ladder propped up and ready for the higher parts of the project. No more projects of that size. At least for now anyway. If only he wasn't so stubborn and would let her help him. Eva mulls the situation over while continuing to watch Bo get his brushes and colors ready. Sea salt is in the air this morning along with an earthy fragrance of the fall foliage. This particular sensory tapestry reminds her she is home.

King Timos strides out, dressed in his ceremonial blue regimentals. The fabric gleams under the sun. Bo squints at him. Eva anticipates Bo's irritation. Maybe her father won't. The King isn't wearing what was planned.

"Timos, I was told you were going to wear earth tones. That's what Eva and Rena requested."

Timos' infectious enthusiasm lights up his eyes. "Nonsense! Blue is my color. It represents the sea, our country's pride."

Bo shakes his head and mutters under his breath. "It'll make you look like a peacock in the painting."

Timos leans in. Eva watches her father tease Bo with an uncharacteristic mischief. "A royal peacock, my friend. A royal peacock." Bo tightens his lips.

Eva walks over, her expression is a mix of amusement and exasperation. "Father, please. We agreed on a more natural palette."

Timos puffs out his chest, places his hand on his hip, and poses to the side. "Royalty must stand out, Eva. You know that."

Bo lifts his paintbrush and points it at Timos while rearranging the paint order with his other hand. "I'll paint you however you want, but if your Queen and daughter revolt, I'm not taking the blame."

Queen Rena glides across the courtyard and joins them. "Timos, do be reasonable. Bo has a point."

Timos sighs a dramatic sigh. "If Bo can wear that hat, I can choose to look like a peacock. Peacocks used to be stylish. I say let's bring the look back."

Bo raises an eyebrow. "Wait. What's wrong with my hat?"

Timos grins. "Nothing, my friend. It's just... unique. Fits you. Like blue. Like blue fits me."

Bo adjusts his Stetson with the top of his paint brush. "It was my granddad's. He wore it while painting. Helps me focus and get in the zone."

Eva's eyes soften. "I didn't know that."

Bo mixes paint. "Yeah, it's kind of a tradition."

"I thought it was part of your style. You know, from the Thirsty Cowboy."

Rena claps her hands to bring them back to the task at hand. "Alright, let's get started before the light changes." She leans over towards Eva. "What's a Thirsty Cowboy?"

Eva laughs with Bo while Bo continues to mix and adjust his paint so he can begin.

Bo begins sketching and the atmosphere lightens. An occasional joke, a light bit of laughter. Still, tension simmers beneath the surface. Rena motions to Eva to follow her inside. She links arms with her mother and make their way indoors. Her mother's voice is quiet, but urgent.

"Eva, don't be upset, but I invited someone here for you to meet. He's waiting for you on the back upper balcony. I've arranged for some refreshments."

Eva pulls her arm away. "*He?*"

"Eva, just settle. We've talked about this before. It's time to move on. You cannot remain single. It's not suitable for a *Princess*." Rena's tone is firm, but kind.

The familiar argument rises between them. "Mother, I'm happy as I am. And I don't have plans to *remain* single, but now is not the time. Please, let's not do this now."

"And he doesn't eat meat? How can a *man* survive and not eat meat. At least eat fish. Does he eat fish?" Rena's rolling questions don't leave a minute for Eva to respond. "Well? Are you going to answer me?"

"Are you done?" Eva's answer is short and pointed.

"What do you mean, am I done?"

"Never mind. Yes, it's true Bo does not eat meat. And no, I'm pretty sure he doesn't eat fish either, although he likes to fish."

"I don't understand, how is this possible?"

"You're right. You probably won't understand." Eva decides to try and move past the interrogation. It will go nowhere fast, anyway.

Rena's eyes narrow slightly. "It's no matter. That's not really what I wanted to talk with you about."

Eva waits a minute to see if her mother is finished. She's not.

"You need to settle down, have children. It's your duty. Lord knows George would have understood." There it is.

Eva can't believe her mother brought him up. "George? Really, you want to talk about George?" That familiar lump beings to swell in Eva's throat. Her patience is wearing thin, if not gone completely. "I understand duties, Mother. But marrying a 'suitable' man isn't on my immediate to do list."

"Well it should be." Rena shakes her head. "I'm sorry if this hurts, but it must be said. I've arranged for you to meet Duke Edward of Zakynthos. You will do this. You will do this for me. He's waiting for you on the balcony. Mind you are respectful, he is of the peerage after all."

Eva groans inwardly. She knows she will not win this battle. It was over before it started. "Fine, I'll meet him. I'll be respectful. That's all."

Eva walks out onto the balcony. Duke Edward sets down his wine glass and rises to greet her. His grandiose presence is slightly overbearing. His lisp is immediately evident when he speaks. "*Princessth* Eva, it *ith* a *pleathure* to meet you." The Duke holds out his hand for Eva to place hers in his as is the custom.

Instead, Eva is quick to cover her mouth to hide her reaction for a moment, before lowering her hand into his to allow him to guide her to the table to join him. "Duke Edward, the pleath— sure is mine."

Edward's enthusiasm bubbles over as he speaks on different topics progressively and lispy with only seconds of breath to spare before ending with his thoughts on plans for his future. "I *thee* a great future for *uth*, my dear, with grand *ballth* and *thelebrathionth*."

Eva struggles to maintain her composure, the exaggerated lisp makes it difficult to take him seriously. "That sounds... delightful, Edward. Wait, what do you mean *us?*"

Edward nods vigorously while a lone lock of hair flops into his eyes. "*Yeth*, your mother and I have spoken and I am aware of your situation. I have no *qualmth* about your *patht*. We *thall* have many children to *thare* our joy."

Eva manages a tight and awkward smile. "I'm sure you're right. But what exactly did you and my mother discuss?" Eva already knows the answer.

As Edward leaves, Eva turns to find her mother waiting by the door. "Well?"

Eva's patience snaps. "Well what, mother?"

"Well, did you and Edward make plans to meet again?"

Eva has had enough. "What do you think? You put me in an impossible situation. Did you see the man as he left?"

Eva watches her mother's expression change from hopeful enthusiasm to dire expectations. "Eva, you didn't."

"I had no choice. I had to undo what you did. I can't marry him. He's... not what I want."

Rena's eyes harden. "You're being unreasonable. Edward is a fine match."

Eva crosses her arms. "You're right. He is. For someone else, but not for me."

Rena's demeanor softens and she turns Eva around and walks her back out onto the balcony. She motions for the servants to clear the table and replenish the wine. "What about Harland, Duke of Rossynthos? You used to adore him."

Eva's heart twinges. Harland. "That was a long time ago. We were just kids."

Rena's eyes twinkle with nostalgia. "It was you, Harland, and Stella as I recall. The three of you went together everywhere. You used to play volleyball on the beach every Spring through early Fall. Am I right?"

A wistful smile forms on Eva's face. "Yes. But things change."

Rena rests her hand gently on Eva's. "Think about it, Eva. I know Harland still cares for you. He's not married and he'd make a good partner."

Eva shakes her head. "I need to make my own choices, Mother."

Rena pulls her hand back into her lap and lifts her glass to her mouth. "Just consider it. That's all I ask."

Eva walks back to Bo and her father in the front courtyard. Her mind is swirling with the weight of her mother's expectations and the reality of her own desires. Bo looks up from his easel. His hat still rests low to shade his eyes. "How'd it go?"

Eva forces a smile. "Let's just say my mother is relentless."

Bo snickers, but his eyes remain serious. "You don't have to do anything you don't want to, Eva."

Eva appreciates his support more than he knows. "Thank you, Bo. The reminder is good to hear."

The sun dips lower, long shadows filter down across the courtyard. Bo's hands move with practiced ease. Her father stays in position seated on a golden throne, just out of earshot. Eva contemplates the differences between their worlds. Differences that loom large creating a chasm that widens with each passing moment.

BO'S FINGERS GRIP THE paintbrush as he works on the portrait of King Timos. The Mediterranean sunlight filters through the large windows of the palace studio, casting a warm glow on the rich, earth-toned drapes and polished marble floors. Bo moved the King inside after he established the background. Now, he can focus on final touches in different lighting. Fresh paint and more salty sea air continues to be the norm. An atmosphere that is both calming and tense. Not unlike the people in his company of late.

King Timos sits in front of him, the regal blue of his ceremonial robes contrasting starkly with the warm autumn palette of the room. Bo's eyes focus on capturing the king's expression, but tension is also there.

"You're doing an excellent job, Bo." Timos' booming voice echoes through the marble-crafted palace .

Bo focuses his attention on the canvas. "Thank you, Your Majesty. I appreciate that."

Timos's tone shifts. He's more serious. "I need to discuss something with you. It's about Eva."

Bo pauses, his heart skips a beat. Here it comes. Honestly he knew it was coming. The writing has been on the wall since they arrived. Subtle, but there. Bo looks up at the King. "Yes, Your Majesty?"

Timos clears his throat and stays still in his pose while speaking. "Eva's future is very important to Queen Rena and me. As you know, she is a Princess. Her duty is to our country and our people."

Bo swallows hard. This conversation is heading exactly where he knew it would. "I understand, Your Majesty."

Timos' lowers his voice and softens, but the underlying firmness remains. "You are a talented artist and a good man, but you must see that Eva's path is different from yours. She needs to marry someone of her rank, someone who can support her in her duties."

Bo's grip on the paintbrush tightens. "Are you saying that you don't approve of my relationship with Eva?"

"Precisely." Timos' gaze is steady and forward. "Queen Rena and I do not see a future for you and Eva together. If you truly love her, you will let her go."

The words hit Bo like a punch to the gut. He stares at his painting, the vibrant colors blur as his vision clouds. "I want what's best for Eva, Your Majesty. But leaving her... it's not easy."

Timos continues in his same tone. "I know. It's difficult. But if you care for her, truly, you must understand that her responsibilities as a Princess come first. Once the portraits are complete, I must ask you to make arrangements to return to Cleveland."

The weight of the King's words settle heavy on Bo's shoulders. "I understand, Your Majesty."

QUEEN RENA AND EVA walk through the lush gardens of the palace. Autumn leaves crunch underfoot. The air is filled with the scent of blooming chrysanthemums and a distant sound of waves crashing against the shore. A soothing backdrop.

"Eva, darling, we need to talk." Rena begins as usual, bright, gentle yet firm.

Eva braces herself for the familiar lecture. "What is it, Mother?"

Rena stops and turns to face her daughter. "It's your future, of course. What about Harland, the Duke of Rossynthos?"

"Of course." Eva rolls her eyes. "Harland, mother? We're just friends. We've always been just friends."

Rena begins cutting some blooms from the chrysanthemums to place in a basket hung on her arm. "Harland is a good man. You two have history together. I've arranged for you to meet him today."

"No! Mother, not today. Please." Eva wanted to set aside some time to spend with Bo. He's been focused on getting the portraits completed and time has been limited. Eva's protests die on her lips. Harland strides across the lawn in her direction. "Mother, you didn't."

"I don't know what you mean, dear."

Tall. Handsome, Harland. His kind smile that reaches his eyes always drew her to him. Comforting. And unsettling. At the same time.

"Eva, it's been too long." Harland envelopes Eva in a warm hug.

"It has, hasn't it?"

Come. Let's sit over hear by the fire pit. The servants just stoked it when they brought out some hot cocoa.

A tall woman with wavy, blond hair catches up with Harland. "Did you tell her?"

"Stella?" Eva would recognize that bold smile anywhere.

Harland pulls his sister to his side. "Can you believe it? She's all grown up."

Stella slaps her brother's shoulder. Eva can't help but notice the tight flex upon impact. Harland. Eva hasn't thought about him in years. Not since before George came into the picture. Stella's eyes sparkle with mischief. "Eva! I just saw what's left of our fort. Remember our secret society days?"

Not that *is* a memory. All the days spent planning and executing adventures all over Tripolia. All over Thalassia. No one was none the wiser. Those were days. "Of course, Stella. And you were the one who came up with the best excursions."

"I know right? She still does. Ask her about Astros." Harland eyes his sister standing by his side with pride and nostalgia.

Eva's heart warms at the memories, but a shadow of doubt lingers. "Astros? What happened at Astros."

Stella and Harland exchange a look. A look that Harland quickly changes to serious. "Astros. That is a story for another day. But today? Today I have other things I want to discuss."

"What things?" Eva's heart pounds in her chest. Her mother. No doubt her mother gave Harland the same spiel as she gave Edward.

Eva glances at Stella who watches her with a knowing look. "What do you think, silly?"

Harland chimes back in. "Our future for one."

Stella grins and spins off into the house. "I think you two would make a great team, just like old times."

Eva's mind races. She thinks of Bo, his passion, his kindness, and the deep connection they share. The love they share for one another. But she also thinks of her duty, her parents' expectations, and the stability someone like Harland could provide. But Bo. She always returns to Bo.

"Eva?" Harland breaks into her thoughts and brings her back to the present moment. She's not sure where she wants to be. Or who she wants to be with.

The sun begins to set over the Mediterranean, casting its familiar red-gold glow over the palace and its gardens. The weight of a decision Eva is going to be forced to make soon presses down on her. She knows she must choose between following her heart with Bo or fulfilling her duties with Harland.

Eva looks at Harland. "I need time to think."

Harland has nothing but understanding in his eyes. "Take all the time you need, Eva. I'll be here when you're ready." He always made her feel safe. Feel secure. Feel sane amid chaos.

Harland kisses her hand as he rises to find Stella so they can head back home. Eva walks back to toward the chrysanthemum patch where she left her mother earlier. Eva's mind is a whirlwind of emotions. The sea and the touch of the evening breeze blend together, grounding her in the present while her thoughts are torn between the past and the future.

IREANNE CHAMBERS

CHAPTER TWELVE

E va moves through the palace halls as the Fall Mediterranean air against her skin reminds her of her life before. Before Bo. Before George. A sharp contrast to the warmth of the sun. Her heart pounds with unease, her mind races with thoughts of Bo. Where is he? Eva hasn't seen him since yesterday when he was working hard to finish the last strokes on the portrait of her father. A sinking feeling in her stomach grows stronger as each moment passes. He needs to get started on her mother's portrait next.

Eva finds her father in the grand library among the richness of aged books and the sharpness of polished wood. "Father, where's Bo? I haven't seen him since last night."

Timos looks up from his book, his expression unreadable. "Eva, I believe Bo has left. He finished his work and decided to return to Cleveland."

"What? He hasn't finished, yet. He still needs to complete mother's portrait. And then mine."

"Your mother and I decided it was best to stop with one portrait."

Eva's heart clenches. "What? What did you say to him? He wouldn't leave without saying goodbye!"

Queen Rena enters the room with her usual elegance and grace just in time to hear the discussion. "Eva, darling, sometimes people leave because they believe it's for the best."

Eva's eyes widen in disbelief. "He wouldn't just leave like that. He loves me. I know he does. And I love him."

Timos closes his book and steadies his gaze on Eva. "Perhaps he realized the difficulties that lie ahead. The differences in your ranks, his condition... He may have felt that he couldn't give you the future you deserve."

Eva shakes her head while tears well up in her eyes. "He wouldn't abandon me without a word. There must be another reason."

Rena steps closer, her voice is gentle but firm with a touch of pomposity. "Eva, it's possible he felt inadequate. Maybe he worried he couldn't father children because of his injury. There are many reasons why he might have left."

A rush of anger and despair exudes from Eva. Sentences starting with her name sets her off. "You think he left because he couldn't have children? That's absurd! He loves me. And how do you know he can't father children? Did you ask him?" As soon as the question flew from her mouth she knew the answer. "Of course you did!"

Timos comes near to her and places a hand on her shoulder. "To answer your question, no. No we did not. But you must know love is not always enough. He must have had his reasons."

"I'm sure you provided him with reasons."

Timos removes his hand and turns back to sit down. "Now Eva, perhaps he simply agreed that it was best for you to find someone who could match your status and fulfill all your needs."

Eva's heart aches with confusion and betrayal. Tears fall good and hard now. "I can't believe he would do it. It doesn't make sense."

Rena steps in to wrap her arms around her daughter. "I understand your pain, darling. Your father and I were an arranged marriage. But look, now we love each other dearly. Maybe Bo thought he was sparing you future heartache. You deserve someone who can stand by your side, someone like Harland."

Eva frowns and looks up at her mother. "Harland?"

"Yes, Harland. You know, the Duke of Rossynthos. He's always cared for you, Eva. He understands our world, our duties."

Eva's anger flares hot. "So, this is your solution? Replace Bo with Harland?"

Rena gives Eva a squeeze. "It's not about replacing anyone, dear. It's about finding someone who can truly be your partner. Harland is of your rank and understands your responsibilities."

More tears escape and roll down Eva's cheek. "You don't understand. Bo and I were happy. He made me happy again after George."

Rena gently wipes Eva's tears away. "We want you to be happy too. But you must have stability. Give Harland a chance. You loved him once."

Eva turns away. Her mother's words are loaded and large. She walks out to the beach adjoining the palace. The sand beneath her feet ground her to reality. Waves crash against the shore in rhythmic and soothing sounds, although still relentless. Eva finds her spot on the sand and sits down with her thoughts swirling like the waves.

Rena joins her by sitting down beside her. "Eva, I know this is hard. But sometimes, the best decisions are the most painful ones."

Eva looks out at the sea, her voice barely above a whisper. "I miss him, Mother. I miss him so much and he's only been gone a day."

Rena wraps an arm around her daughter. "I know, darling. But you're strong. And you have people who love you and want the best for you."

Eva takes a deep breath, salt air fills her lungs. She lays her head on her mother's shoulder. "I'm not ready. I'm not ready to give up that quick. It feels like George again, only worse. So much worse."

Rena strokes the side of Eva's hair and gives her a kiss right over her ear. "No one expects it to be easy."

The sun begins to dip below the horizon as a flicker of hope amidst her sorrow. Eva knows the path ahead will be difficult. It's not the first time she has been subjected to loss. But she also knows she must move forward. For herself, for her family, and for the memory of the love she shared with Bo. Eva makes a silent promise to herself. She will honor that love by living fully and embracing the opportunities before her. She will give Harland a chance, not to replace Bo, but to create a new chapter in her life. A new chapter with possibilities and hope. Hope.

In the Winter, Cleveland, Ohio, U.S.A.

BO'S BREATH CATCHES in his throat as he wheels himself out of the arrival gate at Cleveland Hopkins Airport. The cold winter air nips at his skin, and the smell of jet fuel and exhaust is strong in the terminal. He forgot about the cold winter months in Cleveland. Thalassia was cool, not frigid. Bo's heart beats hard in his chest. The last days of his time in Thalassia press down on him. Eva overwhelms his thoughts. He scans the crowd and spots Don's tall frame and Greta's waving hand.

Don strides forward with a broad smile on his face. "Bo! Good to see you, man."

Bo forces a smile. "Good to see you too, Don. Greta."

Greta leans down and gives him a warm hug. "Welcome back, Bo. We missed you."

Don takes the handles of Bo's wheelchair and pushes him back into the terminal to the baggage claim. "Let's get your baggage and get you home. How was Thalassia?"

Images of Eva invade Bo's thoughts, again. He looks out at the snow-dusted tarmac. "Beautiful place. Not so beautiful memories."

Don frowns. "What happened? Why did you leave so suddenly? I thought you'd be there at least till Spring."

Bo's eyes cloud over. "King Timos and Queen Rena. They asked me to leave. Said it was best for Eva. And best for me. Our differences in rank... They're right, it would never work."

Greta sighs. "I'm so sorry. Eva must be heartbroken."

Bo's throat tightens. "I couldn't even say goodbye."

Don and Greta help Bo into his truck. Worn leather and pine air freshener envelope him. "What did you do in here, Don? What's with the pine smell?" Don ignores him and starts the engine. It's soothing rumble changes Bo's focus. Yes, soothing, yes bittersweet.

"Thirsty Cowboy has been busy." Don changes the silence into words. "Lots of new talent coming through."

Bo works hard to listen. To remember the comfort of home. "That's good. Have you been to the Art Museum since I left?"

Greta chimes in. "They had a great exhibit last month. Local artists. You would have loved it."

Bo's heart twinges. "I wish I could've seen it."

Don glances at Bo in the rearview mirror. "So, have you changed your mind about the surgery?"

Bo's gaze drifts out the window, watching the snowflakes dance in the air. Not a topic he wishes to discuss. "No. My decision hasn't changed. My life has changed. My art and my music. That's my life."

Don keeps Bo in his sights at random intervals. "Alright. We hear you. Whatever is good for you."

"I appreciate that, Don. Truly."

They pull up to Bo's house and Winter swells bite as they step out. The sounds of home— honking cars, distant sirens— a stark contrast to the serene blue of Thalassia.

Inside, Bo feels the warmth of home wrap around him. Don and Greta help him settle, their colorful banter is a soothing balm to his weary soul.

Greta hands Bo a beer. "You'll get back to your routine in no time. You've got this."

Bo tips the bottle back and enjoys a gulp of his go-to Killian's Irish Red. Smooth and dark. "Thanks, Greta."

Don sits across from Bo and takes a gulp of his own bottle. His expression turned serious. "So, what exactly is your next move?"

Bo looks around the room. A room filled with his paintings and memories. "I'll keep painting. Maybe do some shows, sell a few pieces. And I'll play at Thirsty Cowboy when I can. I might pursue a recording deal somewhere down south. I always wanted to check out Nashville."

A glint of pride forms in Don's eyes. "Sounds like a good plan. Yep, a good plan, man." Don gulps down another swig of his beer.

Bo's heart swells with gratitude. "Thanks, Don. I don't know what I would do without you guys."

The night wears on. Stories and laughter. The warmth of friendship. Yet, as Bo lies in bed that night, a cold reality of his situation settles in. King Timos' words haunt him. The thought of Eva brings a fresh wave of sorrow.

But as the first light of dawn filters through the window, Bo decides he will focus on what he loves. His art. His music. His life. His life he has built here. Disabled, but not without strength. Not without endurance. Not without hope. He may have left Thalassia behind, left Eva behind, but he carries the memories, the lessons, and her love in his heart.

IREANNE CHAMBERS

CHAPTER THIRTEEN

In the Spring, City of Tripolia, Country of Thalassia

Eva paces her room. A Spring breeze flutters the lace curtains. Blooming rosemary drifts in while her mind is consumed with Bo. Her phone buzzes in her hand—another unanswered call. She dials again, listening to the endless ringing. Voicemail, again. It can't be the distance. Cleveland is not some small-town outlier. It's a full-blown City!

Click! "Bo, it's Eva. Please, call me back. I need to talk to you."

Eva sends another text, her fingers tremble on each tap. Naz might have some news.

"Naz, have you heard from Bo? I can't get through to him."

Naz texts back. "No joy, honey. He's avoiding everyone. I'm so sorry."

Eva sinks onto her bed, frustration and heartbreak swirl inside her. The door creaks open, and her mother, Queen Rena, pops her head in. "Eva, dear, any news?" Rena's presence is calm and composed. She walks through and sits beside her daughter.

Eva shakes her head and her voice quivers. "Nothing. He's not answering my calls or texts. Even Naz can't reach him."

Rena pats Eva's hand. "Perhaps he needs time, dear. And you know your father. His words may have made him feel unworthy, poor soul."

Pour soul!? Now she cries 'poor soul?' Eva's eyes fill with tears. "Why would Bo do this to me? He said he loved me. And father. Why would *he* do this to me? Doesn't *he* love me?"

"*Ela dé*! You know your father is a man of no words. He loves you. And you should know by now that sometimes love means making difficult choices. Your father only wants what's best for you. Maybe Bo feels the same, have you thought of that?"

Eva pulls away and stands up moving to the window. "And what's best for me is losing the man I love? After I finally found love after George?"

Rena follows Eva to the window and places her hand on Eva's shoulder. "Maybe it's time to consider moving on. Harland is a good man. He's always cared for you."

Eva turns with anger and sorrow building stronger with each minute. "Harland, again! I can't just replace Bo with Harland."

"No one is asking you to *replace* anyone. Just give Harland a chance. I want you to be happy, my dear."

Eva's resolve weakens, she's tired and worn inside. "I'll talk to Harland because we've always been friends. But it won't change how I feel about Bo."

"That's all I ask."

EVA WALKS THROUGH THE woods surrounding the palace. Harland matches steps beside her. He came as soon as she called. Not like someone else she's trying to get through to. Pine and earth scents are strong this time of the year. Eva finds it difficult to believe it has been almost six months since she has seen Bo. He still dominates her thoughts. Most of the time. Birds chirp and pine needles rustle on the ground where they walk. Peaceful. The ruins of the fort they built as children comes into view up ahead, memories flood Eva's mind. Memories of innocence. Memories of hope. Memories of being on top of the world with nothing to lose.

Harland's hand in hers is comfortable, almost normal. "Remember when we thought this fort would protect us from anything?"

Eva allows herself to think about how protected she felt then, and oddly, how protected she feels now. With Harland. "We were so determined. Spent all summer building it."

"And all it took was one storm to bring it down."

Eva looks up at the sky through the fort's 'open ceiling.' "It's not all down. There are still four walls."

"Barely." Harland shoves the wooden plank to prove his point. It doesn't fall. He rolls a fallen log around to position it better for them to sit on. Harland scans Eva's face, his expression is serious. "Eva, I know you're hurting."

Eva clasps her fingers together in front of her and rests her elbows on her knees. "I miss him, Harland. I don't understand why he left without saying goodbye. I don't understand why he's not returning my calls or texts. Or even Naz's calls or texts."

Harland reaches across to take Eva's hand. His touch is calming. "Maybe he thought he was doing the right thing. Sometimes people leave to protect the ones they love."

Eva looks over at Harland searching for answers. "I don't know how to move on from this."

"You don't have to move on. Not until you're ready. I'll still be here."

Dear Harland. A flicker of reminiscence tugs at Eva's heart. "Thank you, Harland. Your friendship means a lot to me."

"I care about you, Eva. I always have."

Harland stands up and offers his hand out to Eva. She places her hand in his and allows him to guide her out of the fort to a nearby stream and they take a seat on a grassy area near the water. Water that flows over rocks, a constant rush of power, a constant power for calm, it begins to lighten the tightness in Eva's chest. The cozy, relaxed presence of a shared history between them provides an element of peace.

"Harland?"

"Hmm?"

"Why did it take this long?"

"What do you mean?"

"I mean, why did you let me marry George? Why now? Why after all these years, you're interested in something more?"

Harland wraps his arm around Eva's shoulders. "Ah. I think that is something you may need to discuss with your father."

It figures. Eva has no interest in hashing out any more from that time period with her father. At least that part of her life can stay there. In the past. Where it belongs. This void, however. This ache that still lurks in her chest when she thinks of Bo? When will that take its place in the past? Harland stands up, it's almost dusk. A whole day with Harland. Pleasant. Surprisingly pleasant.

COUNTESS WHO KISSED A COUNT

CHAPTER FOURTEEN

In the Summer, City of Tripolia, Country of Thalassia

Eva stands in front of her full-length mirror, assessing her reflection with a critical eye. The cream-colored walls adorned with golden accents frame the background for her reflection. If only she could feel the same opulence and comfort in her own reflection that she does when she looks around her room at the palace. Eva turns around and walks out onto the balcony through a large window that also serves as a door. A familiar view of the Mediterranean Sea. Breathtaking. The summer sun casts its glow over everything Eva turns her face up to the sun to enjoy its warmth. Her heart begins to race as she thinks about the beach outing with Harland, her childhood friend, and now the Duke of Rossynthos. When did that start becoming a thing?

Queen Rena enters her room without even a knock, her presence commanding yet nurturing. She's carrying a selection of swimsuits, ranging from elegant one-pieces to daring bikinis. "Eva, darling." Her tone is gentle but firm. "You can't possibly wear that eyesore of a suit to the beach. It's too... well, conservative."

Eva brushes her fingers over the modest swimsuit she is wearing. Too conservative? "Mother, I don't feel comfortable in a bikini. I feel... I don't know a little too chunky, maybe?."

"Nonsense, Eva. You have a beautiful figure. It's not healthy to wear a wet bathing suit on your belly. Trust me." She holds up a vibrant turquoise bikini. "This will look stunning on you, and it's perfect for the occasion. And you'll be happy to know I think that purple lock you try to hide will go perfect with it so untuck it from under your hair, dear. There's no use trying to hide it. Everyone knows you have it. Including your father."

Eva hesitates. It's unlike her father to not vocalize those things he considers unacceptable. She takes the bikini and holds it up against her as if it's going to cover anything. "I'll try it. But no promises."

As Eva changes, Queen Rena continues, "I've instructed the servants to prepare a lovely picnic for you and Harland. Fresh fruits, cheeses, and a light rosé. Everything you need for a perfect day."

Eva emerges from behind the changing screen, exposed but bolstered by her mother's encouragement. "How do I look?"

"Absolutely radiant," Queen Rena smiles, adjusting the purple strand of Eva's hair. "Now, let's talk about makeup. A light touch will do. You want to look natural, not overdone."

Eva nods, applying a subtle layer of makeup under her mother's watchful eye. They choose delicate pearl earrings and a simple bracelet to complete her look. As she finishes, a servant knocks and announces Harland's arrival.

Eva pulls on her lace cover up. Her heart flutters as she descends the grand staircase. This is a new experience. Eva is not accustomed to feeling like this for anyone but Bo. Harland waits at the bottom, looking dashing in his casual beach attire. His smile broadens when he sees her. "Eva, you look stunning."

"Thank you, Harland," Eva's cheeks flush slightly. "Shall we?"

The two make their way to the private beach, the salty breeze carrying the scent of the sea and the sound of gentle waves. The golden sand warms their feet as they walk, and the sparkling water stretches out before them like an endless blue canvas.

They set up near the water a luxurious lounge area shaded by a canopy. Harland opens the picnic basket, revealing the delightful spread prepared by the palace staff. They share a meal, laughing and reminiscing about their childhood antics.

"Remember the time we played volleyball, and you accidentally spiked the ball into old Mrs. Dimitriou's lounge chair just missing the back of her head?"

Eva's light and carefree laugh builds her confidence. "How could I forget? She chased us with her beach paddles all the way to the harbor!"

As they continue their conversation, the bond between them grows stronger with each shared memory. Eva finishes her cucumber and tomato salad and picks up her wine to take a sip.

"It's hot. I'm ready to hit the water again, you?"

"Absolutely!"

The water is warm and the waves are gentle and relaxing. Eva floats and treads water next to Harland. They drift around together and talk about different things they love about summer. A jellyfish drifts by and Eva catches sight of it's almost transparent features. Without missing a beat, Eva maneuvers herself close to Harland and without thinking presses her bikini-clad body to his bare chest, all while wrapping her arms around his neck.

"Don't worry, I've got you." Harland matches her pace as he brings her back to the beach and lays her down on the double lounger bed. His proximity ignites a spark in Eva. A new kind of spark. Not exactly the same as it was with Bo, but a spark.

Eva's pulse quickens, her emotions are a whirlwind of confusion and clarity. She looks into Harland's eyes, seeing a depth of feeling she hadn't noticed before. "Harland, I..."

Harland places a gentle finger on her lips. "Eva, I know this is complicated. But I need you to know how I feel." His voice is tender, filled with earnest emotion. "I've always cared about you, and these past weeks have only made my feelings stronger."

Eva's heart aches with the weight of her own emotions. "I care about you too, Harland. But Bo... I feel like I can't just ignore that part in me."

"Let me see if I can help with that."

Harland leans in. Eva's insides are doing three hundred and sixty degree donuts. She's not entirely sure if she should allow it to happen, but she does. Harland's lips brush hers in a sweet, tangy, and tender kiss. Their tongues touch, soft and tentative.

Eva's mind races, torn. She loves Bo. She's beginning to love Harland. But, in a different way than before. Harland deepens their kiss. Eva allows herself to get lost in the moment, savoring the warmth and tenderness of his touch. For now, under the golden Mediterranean sun, Eva lets herself believe that her heart has room for both.

In the Summer, Medina, Ohio, U.S.A.
BO SITS AT A CORNER table in the Thirsty Cowboy with his guitar propped against the table beside him. The dim

lighting casts a warm, amber glow over the bar, and the air hums with the buzz of conversations and the clinking of glasses. He's just finished his set, a new country ballad that left the crowd cheering, but his heart feels heavier than usual tonight.

Don and Greta join him, their faces lit with pride and affection. Don slaps Bo on the back, a grin splitting his face. "Man, you killed it tonight. That new song... something else."

Greta's eyes shine. "It was beautiful, Bo. You've got a real gift."

Bo smiles, though it doesn't quite reach his eyes. "Thanks, you two. Means a lot."

The waitress brings over a round of drinks, and Bo takes a long sip of his whiskey, savoring the burn as it slides down his throat. The taste is sharp. The familiar scent of sawdust and old wood that fills the bar.

Don's phone buzzes, and his expression shifts from casual to serious in an instant. "Hey, Bo... have you seen this?"

He hands the phone to Bo, the screen displays a social media post from Thalassia's royal family. King Timos and Queen Rena are beaming, and beside them stands Eva, her hand intertwined with a tall man with brown hair and a perfect smile. The caption calls him Harland, Duke of Rossynthos and announces their engagement.

Bo's heart feels like a clamp just closed down on it and a stab shoots through him. He stares at the screen, his mind struggles to process the image. Eva, engaged. To Harland. The Duke of Rossynthos.

"Bo, you okay?" Greta's voice is soft and concerned.

He shakes his head, the noise of the bar fades into the background. "I... I didn't know."

Don places a hand on his shoulder. "Man, I'm sorry. It was a reaction. I shouldn't have showed you. You shouldn't have had to find out like this."

Bo's emotions swirl, a storm of anger, betrayal, and heartbreak. What did he expect? It's not like he had any control over their situation. What else did he expect her to do? She's a Princess! And her parents are the King and Queen. Bo downs his drink, the alcohol doing little to numb his senses. He calls to the waitress. "Another round."

The evening progresses and Bo sinks deeper into his drink. The ache in his chest is persistent. At least he knows that's not paralyzed. He scans the bar and his eyes land on a woman standing alone near the jukebox. Desperation and anger fuel his next move.

He wheels himself over and his voice slurs. "Hey, you lookin' for company?"

The woman's eyes flicker with discomfort. "Um, no, thanks."

Bo's smile is bitter. "Figures."

Don appears beside him with an expression of concern and frustration mixed. "Bo, come on. This isn't you."

Bo glares at him, his insides are boiling over. "What do you know, Don? You're not stuck in this chair, watching the woman you love get engaged to someone else."

Greta approaches. "Bo, c'mon. Let's just get you home."

Bo's eyes narrow and he wheels himself toward the door, heading for his recently acquired van. "I can drive myself. Just make sure to get my guitar before you leave."

Don steps in front of him, blocking his path. "No, you can't. Do you remember what put you in that chair?"

The reminder hits Bo like a punch to the gut, sobering him slightly. He slumps in his chair, the fight drains out of him. "I just... Don. I love her."

"I know, man. But getting drunk won't help. Let's go home.."

The weight of Bo's grief settles over him like a heavy blanket. Don helps him into the van, ensuring he's secure before getting behind the wheel. Greta climbs in beside him, offering quiet support.

They drive through the quiet streets of Medina and onto the highway toward Bo's house. The hot night air of Cleveland Summers does little to alleviate Bo's turmoil inside. He gazes out the window, the dark shadows blur past, his mind replays the image of Eva and Harland over and over.

IREANNE CHAMBERS

CHAPTER FIFTEEN

Bo sits in his wheelchair, staring out the window. The summer heat presses against the glass, making the world outside shimmer like a mirage. His fingers drum on the armrest with a rhythm of frustration and despair. Don paces the room. The floor creaks under his restless footsteps.

"I don't understand why you won't fight for her." Don's voice cracks like the ice in Bo's untouched glass of lemonade.

Bo's jaw tightens. "Because it's over. The King made his wishes clear. And no one goes against the King. She's with Harland now. "

The doorbell rings in a sudden, sharp sound that cuts the air. Don opens the door. Rose and Hank, each holding a suitcase stand on the doorstep. Their tie-dye shirts and worn jeans are a stark contrast to the somber mood in the room.

"Surprise!" Rose's voice is a burst of sunshine in the gloom.

Bo's heart twists. "What are you doing here?"

"Are you going to invite us in?"

"Do I have a choice?"

Rose and Hank walk in and Hank sets down his suitcase and walks over, placing a hand on Bo's shoulder. "We heard the news."

A strong scent of patchouli follows Rose as she moves closer. "We're not letting you go through this alone, Bo."

Bo swallows hard, his throat is dry. "I appreciate that, but—"

"No buts." Rose interrupts in the way only a mother can. "We're going to stay until you're back on your feet."

"Really, mom? You had to say that?" Bo's frustration is enhanced by a cloud of everything's-gonna-be-alright singing in his head. It's not going to be alright.

"You know what I mean, honey. It's just an expression."

Don crosses his arms and eyeballs Bo. "They're right, man. You can't just sit here and wallow."

Bo's eyes sting and he blinks rapidly. "What do you expect me to do? She's marrying someone else."

Hank kneels beside Bo. "You have a gift. Your art, your music... use them."

Rose nods, her hand warm on Bo's arm. "Channel your pain into your work. Document your journey with Eva. Paint it all, from start to finish."

Bo's fingers twitch. The thought of painting again stirs something inside him, a flicker of purpose in the darkness. "You think that'll help?"

Rose's eyes shine with unshed tears. "I know it will. Art has always been your refuge."

Hank stands steady. "And we'll be here every step of the way. I said that on purpose. You can still take steps, even from a wheelchair."

Bo's heart hungers with a mix of gratitude and sorrow. He looks at Don, then back at his parents. "I don't know man."

Don steps forward, placing a hand on Bo's shoulder. "Yes!"

The room falls silent. The significance of what and who surrounds him and presses from the inside out. Bo takes a deep breath. He knows they're right. "Okay. I'll paint."

Rose's smile is like the first light of dawn. "That's the spirit, my boy."

Hank grins, clapping Bo on the back. "You won't regret it son."

Bo's heart does laps in his chest with a mixture of fear and determination coursing through him. "I'll paint our story." One brush stroke at a time. One step forward. He can almost taste the possibility of healing and the bitterness of loss giving way.

In the Summer, City of Tripolia, Country of Thalassia
EVA RIDES ALONGSIDE Harland on the palace grounds, the landscape is spiced with wildflowers. The sea breeze salts the air. Horses' hooves drum a steady rhythm against the earth.

"This place is breathtaking." Harland glances over at Eva, his eyes crinkle with his smile. "Almost as much as you."

Eva's blush creeps warm up her neck. She's still not used to this new kind of relationship with Harland. "You always know what to say."

"Only because it's true." He looks at the area around them. "Do you ever get tired of this view?"

Eva shakes her head, a light breeze wisps her hair across her face. "Never. It's home."

"I hope you'll feel the same way about our home."

Eva's heart skips a beat. "Our home?"

"Yes. Our home. Once we're married."

The gravity of his words settle over Eva. Bo drifts through her thoughts. His smile, his kindness, his thoughtfulness. Eva pushes the memories aside, intent to focus on the man trotting beside her.

As they reach a scenic overlook, Harland dismounts and helps Eva from her horse. The sea stretches out to the horizon, shimmers like diamonds under the sun's rays. Harland takes her hand, his touch sends a shiver down her spine. Not exactly the way Bo touched her, but enough. And much better than George.

Harland wraps his arm around Eva's waist. "This is where I see our future."

Eva's heart swells with emotion. Harland pulls her close, his breath is warm against her cheek. "Eva, I want to make you happy. I want to give you everything."

Eva's eyes flutter shut as his lips brush hers, a gentle caress that quickly deepens. Eva melts into his embrace, her body responding to the heat of his touch.

Harland's hands travel over her back, his fingers trace the curve of her spine. Eva's mind spins, the world narrows to the sensations coursing through her.

"I want you, Eva. I need you."

Eva's heart pounds, the voice of reason resonates in her mind. Bo resonates in her mind. "Harland, we should wait. Until we're married."

"We're getting married, Eva. It's just a matter of time."

"I know, but it's important to me. To wait."

Harland's eyes search hers, a flicker of frustration gives way to understanding. "Okay. We'll wait."

A rush of relief and gratitude streams through Eva's core. "Thank you."

He kisses her gentle on the lips. "Anything for you."

They stand there for a moment longer enjoying the diorama, the intensity of their embrace ebbs into a peaceful closeness. The sea and the chirping of birds surround them.

Harland's hand tightens around her. "Shall we head back?"

"Yes, let's."

They dismount once they are closer to the stables and walk a short distance with the horses trailing behind them. The sun is lower in the sky now. Long shadows permeate the palace grounds. Hay and leather aromas greet them the closer they get.

Harland turns to Eva. "I want you to know, Eva, that I love you. More than anything."

Eva's heart aches, a little bittersweet. "I love you too."

He kisses her forehead. "We'll make a wonderful life together."

Eva's thoughts continue to stray to Bo, to the love they shared. She pushes the memories down and focuses again on the man who stands before her. "I believe we will."

As they walk back to the palace, Eva tries to silence the doubts in her heart. She loves Harland, of that she's certain. But the shadow of her feelings for Bo still lingers, a constant reminder of the love she's trying to leave behind.

Harland's voice breaks into her thoughts. "What are you thinking about?"

Eva looks up, meeting his gaze. "Just about how thankful I am to have you."

Harland's smile shines with affection. "And I you, Eva."

Eva's eyes fill with tears, moved by his sincerity. Her heart still yearns for someone who doesn't want her. Harland pulls her into a hug, the strength of his embrace is a comforting anchor. Eva clings to him, hoping that in time, her heart will follow the path her mind has chosen.

COUNTESS WHO KISSED A COUNT

CHAPTER SIXTEEN

In the Fall, Cleveland, Ohio, U.S.A.

B o squints at the canvas, his brush moves with swift precision. Sunlight pours through the large windows of his art studio. Hues of dark and light splash across the wooden floor. His usual linseed oil and acrylic paint hang in the air. Bo's Stetson hat, a symbol of his roots and resilience, rests on a stool nearby.

Bo steps back from his latest canvas, wiping a streak of red paint from his cheek. "Don, you should see this." His voice echoes through the spacious room.

Don leans against the doorway. "Another masterpiece, Picasso?" His leather jacket creaks as he crosses his arms.

"Not quite." Bo laughs at his friend's reaction. "But it's something." He gestures to the painting. A vivid depiction of Eva stumbling into the coffin in the corn maze, where he had been dressed as Count Dracula. The colors are bold, capturing the chaos and surprise of that moment.

Don steps closer and squints. "Man, I remember that night. She screamed so loud I thought my eardrums would burst."

Bo snickers rich and full. "Yeah, and I thought I'd have a heart attack." Best to keep why he almost had a heart attack to himself.

"You're a glutton for punishment, you know that? Although you do have a certain... charm in a cape." Don's eyes sparkle with mischief.

Bo's smile fades a bit as he traces the lines of Eva's figure in the painting. "It was a good night. One of the best. I think that was the moment I fell for her. In that stupid corn maze." More thoughts about that night flare up.

Don claps a hand on Bo's shoulder. "You've captured it perfectly, buddy. It's all there—her shock, your ridiculous cape. It's like stepping back in time. And yeah. I'd say you were hook, line, sinker, and fly on a line." And everything in between although Bo chooses to keep the "everything" to himself. No one else needs to know.

"Thanks, Don. It means a lot to hear that." Bo shifts, picks up a brush, and adds a final touch of orange to the painting. The scene feels complete now, a snapshot of a happier time.

"What's next in the collection?"

Bo grins, the corners of his eyes crinkle. "The accident, believe it or not. It's part of the journey, right? Can't leave it out."

Don winces. "True. It's all part of the story. Just... make sure you paint the recovery too. People need to see that."

Bo's eyes gleam, determined. "Absolutely. Recovery is the best part."

BO SITS IN HIS COZY living room, the plush cushions of the couch support his tired body. Freshly brewed coffee mixed with vanilla from a burning candle on the coffee table remind him he has company.

Rose and Hank open the front door with groceries in their hands rustling with excitement. "Bo, we heard the news! A record deal in England? That's incredible!" Rose drops the bags to the side and clasps her hands together in joy.

Bo beams. "Yeah, it's surreal. I never thought my country ballads would resonate over there, but here we are. And who was it that emptied their hat?"

Rose giggles as she plants a kiss on her son's cheek. "It was Greta. I saw her at the salon. I'm glad to know you still remember things I teach you."

"Of course I remember. I used to love 'spilling beans' from my hat when you made us guess secrets and I won."

Hank picks up the bags of groceries and puts them on the table. "That's because I let you win."

"Yeah, I realized that the older I got."

Hank leans forward, pride is evident in his gaze. "You've got a gift, Bo. People recognize that, no matter where they are."

"Thanks, Dad." Bo's voice is infused with gratitude. "But there's a bit of a hiccup. I need a lawyer who knows about immigration and entertainment law."

Rose's eyes light up. "Naz! Naz would be perfect for this! She's experienced, and she's got that fire you need in a lawyer. She'll make sure everything is handled."

Bo creases up. "How do you know Naz?"

"Oh, I met her once, somewhere. Maybe through Greta?"

"How does Greta know her?" Bo begins to squirm on the sofa, a movement more fluid than it has been in a long time. "You know what? Never mind. It doesn't matter. I'll give Naz a call tomorrow."

BO SITS IN A COZY CAFÉ, with a fireplace, plenty of coffee and tea and cider, presumably Naz's office. Chatter and clinking cups create the backdrop. Bo pulls his Stetson down slightly in the front. Journey and resilience.

Naz walks in and immediately puts him at ease. She pulls up a chair next to him with eyes bright and curious. "Bo, it's so good to see you. How are you holding up?"

"I'm doing well, Naz. Better than I expected, honestly."

Naz's gaze eases any tension and her eyes reflect empathy and admiration. "I've heard about your art collection. It sounds incredible. Capturing your journey with Eva through your paintings... that's powerful."

Bo's fingers tracing the rim of his cup. "It's been therapeutic, in a way. Painting helps me process things. And now, with this record deal in England, it feels like a lot of things are falling back into place."

Naz's lips expand into a smile . "That's amazing, Bo. Your music, your art, they touch people. You inspire more people than you know."

"Thanks, Naz." A warm flush of gratitude warms Bo's cheeks.

Bo explains the details of the record deal while Naz's expertise shines through as she outlines the steps they'll need to take. Her confidence and knowledge instill calm. Bo is in good hands.

Naz leans back, thoughtful and sips her coffee. "You know, your story is remarkable. This is an incredible art and music journey... it's inspiring and gripping."

Bo's heart swells with a mixture of emotions. "It's been a wreck of a ride, that's for sure. It's become an intense part of who I am now."

Naz reaches across the table and gives his hand a gentle squeeze. "And who you are is pretty amazing, Bo. Don't ever forget that."

Bo's gratitude swells into something more— a sense of connection that goes beyond words. "Thank you, Naz."

Naz smiles, a small twinkle in her eye. "By the way, I'll be attending Eva's wedding. Just a heads-up."

Bo falters slightly inside, but he quickly recovers. "That's great. I hope it goes well for her."

Naz becomes serious. "Bo, if there's anything you might want me to do—"

Bo shakes his head. "No. Nothing about me or our conversations should be mentioned. I'm trusting you. Attorney/client privilege is what I think you call it?"

Naz purses her lips. "Understood. But just so you know, I think Eva is missing out on something wonderful."

Bo's laugh is tinged with a hint of sadness. "Maybe. But we all have our paths, I guess."

"Right. And yours, my friend, is looking pretty bright from where I'm standing."

The conversation drifts to lighter topics. Peace and anticipation for the future begin to well up inside him. A long and painful journey is now peppered with moments of joy and growth.

IREANNE CHAMBERS

CHAPTER SEVENTEEN

In the Fall, City of Tripolia, Country of Thalassia

Eva stands on her balcony, the sea breeze lifts tendrils of her hair as she gazes out over the expanse of the palace grounds with a distant call of seagulls floating in the air. Her wedding dress shimmers in the late afternoon sun, a blend of ivory and lace that feels both heavy and light on her shoulders. Eva takes a sip of champagne to calm her nerves, the bubbles dance on her tongue.

Naz stands beside her and scans the horizon. "It's beautiful here. Perfect day for a wedding."

Eva forces a smile, her heart is heavy. "Yes, perfect." She places her glass down and turns to Naz, her dress still shimmers in the sunlight. "Naz, I have to ask you something."

"Of course, Eva. What's on your mind?"

Eva hesitates, then takes a deep breath. "Did you ever talk to Bo about why he left? Why he never said goodbye? Why he wouldn't answer my calls or texts?"

Naz's eyes flicker. "Eva, maybe this isn't the best time..."

"Please, Naz. I need to know. I need to know before I marry Harland." Eva's voice trembles with desperation.

Naz sighs and sets her glass down. "King Timos told Bo to leave. He thought it was best for both of you. Bo believed he was doing the right thing by not saying goodbye."

Eva's eyes widen, her heart pounding in her chest. "I knew it. I knew it was something my parents said or did."

"I tried, Eva. It wasn't until Bo contacted me for legal advice that I learned the whole story. I'm sorry I didn't tell you sooner. I may even regret telling you now."

Eva feels a mix of anger and sadness. She turns away and grips the balcony railing. "All this time, I thought he just left because he didn't love me anymore."

"No, Eva. He loved you. I think he still does."

Eva takes a deep breath, the salty air fills her lungs. "I need to talk to Harland. Now. Before the ceremony."

Naz picks up her glass again, understanding. "Do what you need to do, Eva."

Eva finds Harland in the grand sitting room, his tall frame elegant in his wedding suit, top hat and all. The rich aroma of polished wood and fresh flowers ripples through the air. "Harland, I need to speak with you. It's important."

Harland looks up, surprise flashes in his eyes. "Eva, the ceremony is about to start. It's not good for the groom to see the bride beforehand."

"Please, Harland. This can't wait."

He studies her face for a moment. "Alright. What is it?"

Eva steps closer, her heart pounds. "Did you know my father asked Bo to leave? Did you know he made him go without saying goodbye?"

Harland's expression darkens. "I did. Your father thought it was best for you, at the time."

"And you went along with it?" Eva's voice rises, tears prickle in her eyes. "You knew how much I loved him, and you said nothing?"

Harland's shoulders sag. "Eva, I love you. I've always loved you. But I also wanted what was best for you. I thought... I thought if Bo left, you'd be able to move on. And you did. Haven't we enjoyed each other's company the last few months?"

Eva shakes her head, tears spill down her cheeks. "I can't marry you, Harland. Not when I still love him. Not when I know the truth of it. It'll be like George all over again. I can't. I can't."

Harland steps forward, his hands gentle on her shoulders and sadness in his eyes. "Eva. My precious Eva." Harland holds her against him. "I love you."

Eva pulls back. "Harland, you know I love you to. But, I can't marry you. Yes, it's different, but not enough."

Harland drops his hands to his sides. "I want you to be happy, truly happy. If that means finding Bo, then go. Find him."

Eva's heart is aching. Aching for Harland. Aching for Bo. Aching for herself. "Oh, Harland. What have I done to deserve you? To deserve your love, your friendship? Even now. I want you to find your person too."

Harland smiles dejected, and pulls her close to place a feather-light kiss on Eva's cheek. "Go, my dear. Love doesn't wait." He releases her shoulders, steps back, and tips his top hat with a bow. "I'll take care of the guests. Go, find your happiness. Find your person."

In the Fall, Cleveland, Ohio, U.S.A.

BO SITS IN THE FAMILIAR café, the sweet scent of fresh baked pastries mixes with hazelnut brews, and a soft hum of conversation.

Naz sits across from him with a mix of professional calm and personal concern on her face. "Bo, your art collection for the upcoming show is impressive. The way you've captured your journey is deeply moving."

Bo smiles, though it still doesn't quite reach his eyes. "Thanks, Naz. The whole process has been therapeutic, putting it all on canvas."

"The art show will be a hit, no doubt. People connect with you and your story, your resilience."

Bo shifts and leans forward. "Naz, tell me about Eva's wedding. How was it?" He tries to keep his voice casual, but the tension in his shoulders betrays him.

Naz hesitates, careful to select her words. "It was... an event. Very grand, as you'd expect."

Bo's heart sinks. He wanted more details, a detail, anything. "She looked happy?"

Naz smiles, but it's strained. "She looked... beautiful. As she always does."

Bo's mind does its paces, a mix of longing and sorrow. "Did she... say anything about me?"

Naz looks away with palpable discomfort evident. "Bo, I can't discuss personal matters. I'm doing some legal work for her and negotiations with her parents."

Bo clenches his fists under the table. "I just need to know if she's okay."

Naz reaches across the table, placing a hand on his. "She's okay. She's finding her way, just like you."

The café door chimes, and Don walks in, his eyes immediately find Bo. He saunters over, clipping his friend on the back. "Hey, buddy. How's it going?"

Naz stands, giving Bo a reassuring squeeze on his shoulder. "I'll leave you two to chat. Take care, Bo."

Bo watches Naz leave before turning to Don. "Hey, man. Sit down."

Don plops into the seat Naz vacated and eyes Bo with concern. "You okay? You look like you've seen a ghost."

Bo sighs and runs a hand through his hair. "Naz was vague about Eva's wedding. It's driving me crazy."

Don frowns and furrows his brow. "I thought you were moving past all that."

"I thought so too." Bo's voice is low, lower than the din of the café. "But hearing about her getting married... it brought everything back."

Don leans back and crosses his arms. "You still love her."

Bo laughs with a bitter tang to his voice. "Always have. Always will."

The café buzzes around them, clinking of cups and quiet chatter form the backdrop to their conversation. Bo's eyes drift to the painting on the wall, a vibrant depiction of a fall landscape, reminding him of his upcoming art show.

"Look," Don breaks the silence. "You've got an art show coming up. Focus on that. And then there's the tour in England, Scotland, and Ireland for your new record. You've got a lot to look forward to."

Bo tries to absorb his friend's encouragement. "Yeah, you're right. The tour is a big deal."

"Of course it is, man. I'm gonna be your roadie, and you're going to crush it. Your music speaks to people, just like your art."

"Thanks, man." Bo waives to a waitress for a refill of cider and Don orders one too.

Don glances at Bo's Stetson hat, then back at Bo. "By the way, how's the therapy going?"

Bo's lips twitch into a small smile. "It's good. I can almost go to the bathroom by myself."

Don throws a napkin at Bo. "Dude, seriously. Didn't need to know that."

"I'm just messing with you. Would you expect anything less?"

Don gulps his hard cider and squints from the burn. "Nope, guess not."

Bo laughs a genuine note of acknowledgment this time. "You know me too well."

Bo leans back knowing his future is uncertain, but for now, he has his art, his music, and his friends. And maybe that's enough.

COUNTESS WHO KISSED A COUNT

CHAPTER EIGHTEEN

B o stands in the center of his new gallery, the polished marble floors gleam under the soft glow of recessed lighting. Fresh white with picture rails holding the exhibits line the open concept room. Champagne and hors d'oeuvres are being offered around the room. Bo adjusts his Stetson hat to allow a shadow over his eyes. The collar of his suit and the fabric are smooth against his skin. His boots are polished to perfection and add a rugged touch to his otherwise sophisticated cowboy appearance.

Naz approaches with a mix of excitement and pride. "Bo, this place looks amazing. The setup is perfect."

"Thanks. Couldn't have done it without you."

Don and Greta arrive and Don's eyes sparkle with mischief as he surveys the high-class event. He nudges Bo. "Champagne, really? I hope you have some beer hidden somewhere."

Bo grins and motions one of the servers to come his way. "Don't worry, I've got you covered." Bo grabs a champagne flute and hands it to Don.

"What's this?"

"Try it."

Don sips the contents first and then smiles at Bo. "Dang! Beer in a champagne glass, I'll take it!"

Bo points to a long table with a black tablecloth set up along the edge near the back of the gallery. "Just head over there whenever you want a refill."

Rose and Hank step into the gallery. Rose's long gray hair is tied back with a colorful scarf and exudes her usual, serene, hippie vibe. Hank, with his bushy gray beard, slicked just a bit, emits kind affection. They make their way to Bo with faces beaming with pride.

Rose hugs Bo tight, a whiff of lavender surrounds her. "Bo, this is wonderful! You did it!"

Hank offers Bo his firm grip for a handshake. "You've come a long way, son. This is just the beginning."

"Thanks, Mom. Thanks, Dad. I'm glad you're here."

Naz stands nearby and takes a sip of her champagne and smiles at the family scene. "Bo, tell me more about the tour. England, Scotland, and Ireland, right?"

Excitement lights up Bo's face. "Yeah, it's going to be incredible. Thanks to your negotiations with Song Music, it's all happening."

Naz grins. "I'm glad it's working out. Another done music deal. I have to tell you, your parents remind me a little of my friend Lucy and her husband King. Lucy has this great Boho style going on. I won't bore you with the details of their adventures, but King's father owns Song Music."

Bo laughs. "That's amazing. I would welcome a chance to hear more of their adventures, though."

Naz's eyes twinkle. "They're quite the pair. How are things going with Rose and Hank living in an RV on your property?"

Bo glances at his parents. "It's been alright. I was unsure at first, but it turns out I like having them around. And, always something interesting is happening with them."

Naz sips her champagne. "I can only imagine."

The gallery hums with the sound of conversation and laughter. Bo's art pieces, each telling a part of his and Eva's story, draw appreciative murmurs from the guests. The circular display leads viewers through their journey from the beginning to the end, capturing the highs and lows with vivid colors and emotional depth.

Naz checks her watch and sighs. "Bo, I have to leave. I have an appointment I can't miss."

Bo raises an eyebrow. "Anything important?"

Naz hesitates, then smiles. "Just something I need to take care of. You'll do great tonight. Enjoy it."

Bo nods with a hint of curiosity in his eyes. "Thanks, Naz. For everything."

As Naz leaves, Don sidles up to Bo, a beer-filled champagne flute in hand. "She's always so mysterious, isn't she?"

Bo *Tsks*. "Yeah, she is. But she's been a huge help."

Don's gaze shifts to the art pieces. "This show... it's really something. You've poured your soul into these."

Bo's eyes soften as he looks at the paintings. "It's our story, Don. I wanted to capture it all."

Don slaps Bo's shoulder. "You did. And now, we've got the tour to look forward to. England, Scotland, Ireland... it's going to be epic."

Bo grins, excitement bubbles up again at the thought of it. "I can't wait. Greta's still on for everyone's stage makeup, right?"

"Yeah, she's thrilled about it. She's already planning the looks. And already marked the time off."

Bo's heart feels full as he takes in the scene around him. "I'm glad you're all coming with me. It's going to be an incredible journey."

Don's expression grows more serious for a moment. "So, I'm guessing the therapy is over?"

Bo's smile remains steady. "It's going better than I expected, it's really helping."

"I'm glad to hear it. Progress. That's what matters."

The evening continues, the gallery fills with people coming and going. Sounds of admiration and joy envelop the room. Bo feels a sense of accomplishment. His journey has been long and challenging, but tonight, surrounded by friends and family, it's all been worth it. He relishes the sight, his heart is light.

"Ready for the tour?" Greta's eyes shine.

A full grin spreads across Bo's face. "More than ready. Let's make some memories."

EVA STEPS OFF THE PLANE at Cleveland Hopkins Airport, the familiar chill of Fall bites her cheeks. The terminal buzzes, luggage wheels clatter, and overhead announcements interrupt in spurts. Coffee and fast food fill the air, a blend of comfort and slightly stale. Eva scans the crowd, her heart races with anticipation. She spots Naz waving from across the terminal. Waving like she always does when Eva visits.

Naz's floral perfume mixes with the airport smells. "Eva, it's so good to see you! How was your flight?"

"Long but smooth. Thanks for picking me up."

Naz takes Eva's luggage and leads her towards the exit. "I've got a surprise for you. We're going somewhere special."

Eva raises an eyebrow. "Not another one of your 'adventures,' I hope?"

Naz laughs, a light, tinkling sound. "Oh, you'll love this one. Trust me."

They walk out into the Cleveland Fall air, the sky is a canvas of orange and pink as the sun begins to set. Leaves crunch underfoot, their rich, woody scent fills Eva's senses and she remembers the last time she was here, also in the Fall. They reach Naz's car and load the luggage into the trunk.

As they drive, Eva glances at Naz. "So, how is Bo? Is he still the same cowboy with his Stetson hat?"

Naz smirks, but keeps her eyes on the road. "You'll see for yourself soon enough."

Eva's heart skips a beat. "Wait, where are we going?"

Naz gives her a mysterious smile. "You'll find out."

Eva narrows her eyes playfully. "Naz, you're always up to something. Does Bo know I'm back?"

Naz shakes her head. "Nope, I haven't told him anything. It's not my place."

A touch of sarcasm fuels Eva's voice. "You always intercede in questionable situations, but this time you're staying out of it?"

Naz glances at her, amusement dances in her eyes. "This time, it's different. You both are my clients."

Eva rolls her eyes. "You know I don't do social media."

Naz chuckles. "I know. But maybe you should start, get with times. You know Bo has a YouTube channel. Anything you might want to know would be there."

Eva scoffs. "I'm not getting with the times. Remember Oxford? The media frenzy? When they found out I was a Princess?"

Naz laughs, shaking her head. "Yeah, I remember. This is different, though. Just trust me."

They pull up to a modern, sleek building with large glass windows. The sign above the entrance reads "Bo MacLachan Art Gallery." Eva's heart leaps into her throat.

Naz turns to her with a grin. "Welcome to Bo's new gallery. Tonight's his opening night."

Eva feels a mix of excitement and nerves. "Naz, you're impossible."

Naz winks. "Come on, let's go."

They step inside, the warmth of the gallery enfolds them. Soft murmurs of conversation and the faint clinking of champagne glasses welcome them first. Floral arrangement speckle the gallery along with servers circulating with flutes of champagne and appetizers creating an inviting and sophisticated atmosphere.

Naz hands Eva a glass of champagne. "Enjoy. I'm going to mingle. Take your time."

Eva takes a sip, the bubbles tickle her nose. She scans the gallery, but there is no sign of Bo. She begins to wander through the gallery. She begins to explore at the end of the room. She stops in front of a painting depicting Bo standing on stage, singing passionately, his Stetson hat and guitar prominent in the front.

Eva's breath catches in her throat. The painting is vibrant and full of life, capturing Bo's essence perfectly. She moves to the next painting. Bo is painting a portrait of her father, King

Timo. The detail is incredible, every brushstroke is filled with intensity. This portrait is different from the original one. This one has a backdrop of red splashed onto the canvas, almost like he's standing in fire. Eva is not unaware of its possible meaning.

The next painting is a serene landscape of her home in Thalassia, the palace and the Mediterranean Sea in the distance. The colors are soft, warm, and floral. A sense of nostalgia creeps in, but not for long.

As she continues, the paintings become more intense. One shows Bo in a hospital, receiving treatment, another shows him in a wheelchair, his face a mix of determination and pain. Eva's heart aches as she takes it all in. She scans the room again. Where is he?

The next painting is a chaotic scene of a wrangled pickup truck the same color of maroon she remembers Bo drove, a bottle of booze, and a drunk man, symbolizing the accident that changed everything. A tear slips down Eva's cheek.

Finally, Eva reaches the last painting. It takes her breath away, if taking someone's breath away is possible. The corn maze. Eva, dressed in what looks like an 18th century ball gown tripping into a coffin. Bo, dressed as Count Dracula. The painting in its whimsical nature is full of humor, yet pure emotional for her. Eva reads the title. "Countess who Kissed a Count."

Tears begin to stream down Eva's face. A masculine presence moves cautious and slow positioning himself beside her.

"You know you started at the end." His masculine voice is familiar.

She turns and gasps. Bo stands next to her, no longer in a wheelchair, and without his Stetson hat. He looks different, but still her Bo. "Bo?"

He smiles, his eyes full of kind essence. "It's me."

Eva jumps closer to him and wraps her arms around him pulling him tight against her. "I can't believe it's really you, standing here, walking!"

Bo holds her close, his scent reminds her of leather and fresh air. "Yes, I am." Bo nuzzles his face into her neck.

Eva pulls back, her eyes searching his. "Why didn't you tell me?"

Bo's voice is gentle. "I didn't want to cause you any more distress."

"Distress? How could you having surgery and walking again cause me distress?"

"I knew your parents didn't approve. And I knew you would go against their wishes. And I didn't want to be the cause of that."

Don and Greta join them, their faces lit with elation. "This is amazing, man. Welcome back, Eva."

Greta hugs Eva warmly. "It's so good to see you."

Bo tangles Eva's fingers in his while they stand side-by-side. The last time they were in a gallery like this was not long before Bo's accident. Now this is Bo's gallery. And here she is standing close to him again. Standing with him by her side. Eva's heart is overwhelmed with the thrill of everything that has happened in the last few days. She's not losing him again. This man, standing by her side. Standing.

BO TAKES EVA'S HAND, feeling the delicate bones beneath her soft skin. He leads her to a secluded bench behind a wall in the gallery, seeking the privacy they desperately need. "Remember the last time we were in an art gallery together?" Bo's eyes search hers.

A wistful smile plays on Eva's lips. "How could I forget?"

Bo sits down, pulling Eva beside him. He hesitates and then asks the question he doesn't want to know the answer to. "Where's Harland?"

Eva sighs, her smile fades. "Harland and I realized we still care for each other, but only as friends."

Bo takes Eva's hand and interlaces his fingers with her. Her soft hair brushes against his cheek. "Eva..." Bo whispers, his voice trembles with emotion. "Wait, what?" Bo pulls back to look at Eva's face. "You mean, you're not married?"

Eva's eyes widen, and she cups his face with her free hand. "Bo, I've always loved you. I couldn't marry Harland because I still in love you."

Bo's heart leaps, but he hides his relief. "I'm sorry, Eva." Even though he isn't.

"But I couldn't understand why you left without saying goodbye and why you wouldn't answer my calls or my texts, but I understand now." Eva's eyes are locked with Bo's.

"What is it that you understand?" Bo's afraid of her answer.

"I understand you were trying to protect me. But love doesn't work that way."

"Oh, no?"

"No. You can't protect someone from loving you, silly."

Bo's insides roil. The good kind. Relief, joy, and love. He leans in, capturing her lips in a kiss that is both tender and intense. Their tongues mingle together, the taste of her filling him with a sense of completeness he has longed for. The world fades away, only the two of them are in this perfect moment.

When they finally pull apart, Bo rests his forehead against hers, their breaths are still one. "Marry me, Bo." she whispers, her voice is filled with hope.

Bo smiles and closes his eyes. "Hey. I'm the one that's supposed to ask you, not the other way around."

Eva presses her lips against Bo's once more. "I'm not losing you again."

Bo immediately kisses her thoroughly pouring all his love and longing into it.

Eva breaks the bond with a teasing glint in her eyes. "There's one problem."

Bo grins, ignoring her words, and kisses her again. "Nope, no more problems."

Eva pushes him back again, playful and urgent. "I have to tell you this, it's important."

Bo clasps his hands around her waist. "Okay, what is it?"

"The Queen insists I be punished for my '*outrageous behavior*' of calling off the marriage to Harland." Eva's eyes are serious.

Bo leans back, his expression turning grave. "Punished how?"

Eva takes a deep breath. "We will have to learn to live on a reduced allowance of only $500,000 a year."

Bo bursts into laughter, relief floods through him. "I can live with that." he pulls her back in for another kiss. The taste of her lips, the scent of her perfume, the feel of her body pressed against his—all of it is perfect.

Eva giggles against his lips, pulling back to look into his eyes. "Bo, I love you."

Bo's heart overflows with happiness. "And I love you, Eva... *my lady*."

IREANNE CHAMBERS

EPILOGUE

Somewhere over the Atlantic Ocean

Bo's private jet hums gently as it glides over the Atlantic. The plush interior rivals a cocoon-filled cylinder of luxury and comfort. Eva sits on the leather sofa, the soft hum of the engines relaxes her. Bo approaches with a mischievous glint in his eyes.

"I have something for you," Bo holds something behind his back.

Eva looks up, curiosity piqued. "What is it?"

Bo reveals a pink, distressed wool Stetson Sedona hat, adorned with a hat band of diamonds and sapphires. "A cowgirl tiara made for my lady." Bo bows slightly as he places the Sedona on Eva's head a proud smile spread across his face. "The distressed look represents the challenges we've faced together, while the bejeweled band is the elegance only my Princess deserves."

Eva's breath catches in her throat. She takes the hat off her head to examine it. Soft worn, wool is exquisite beneath her fingertips. "Bo, it's beautiful." She places the hat back on her head and pulls her cowboy's face toward hers to plant a kiss on his lips, but not before knocking Bo's Stetson with hers.

Bo laughs. "Here, let me show you how it's done." Bo removes Eva's hat and firmly kisses her on the mouth and then places the hat back on her head. Bo's eyes soften as he looks at her. "You look perfect."

A burst of laughter from the other side of the cabin draws their attention. Don and Greta are huddled together, reviewing footage on Greta's camera.

"Hey, Bo," Don calls out and waves them over. "Come check this out."

Eva and Bo join them, and Greta turns the camera to show Bo performing on stage in Scotland. "Your latest YouTube post has gone viral." Greta whoops. "And I have to say, my filming skills deserve some credit."

Bo leans over to get a better view. "Greta, you did an amazing job. But next time, try not to cut off my head."

Greta swats Bo. "Noted. And Eva, are you ever going to join us on social media? Your handsome husband is the star, after all."

Eva shakes her head with a tight-lipped smile. "Nope. I'm happy to leave the spotlight to Bo."

Don snorts. "The Queen of Thalassia, a spectator. Now that's a headline."

"The Queen is my mother, Don."

Bo throws a napkin at Don. "Get it together, bro! You're about to meet them. At least get their titles right."

The cabin door opens, and Rose and Hank stroll in, looking as carefree as ever. Hank's tie-dye shirt clashes with the elegant decor, but he wears it with pride. Rose's long hair flows freely, a stark contrast to Eva's neatly styled locks.

"We brought snacks!" Rose announces, holding up a basket of homemade granola bars and gummies. Earthy scents of oats, honey, and something else follows them through.

Bo grins at his parents. "Thanks, Mom. But remember, we're meeting King Timos and Queen Rena soon. Try not to overwhelm them too much with your... hippie charm."

Rose waves a hand dismissively. "Oh, please. Your Queen mother-in-law can't possibly have an issue with us. She might even enjoy a toke herself."

Bo shakes his head with a smile on his face. "Not on the plane, Mom."

Hank pulls out a pack of blanks and begins the process of rolling a joint looking up as he does, more than a little sheepish. "Right, right. We'll keep it clean."

Don nudges Eva. "What do you think will happen if your parents got high?"

Eva imagines her regal parents in a haze of smoke, giggling uncontrollably. She laughs, shaking her head. "I don't even want to think about it."

Greta leans in, her eyes twinkling. "So, Bo's a vegetarian, and you're a carnivore. How does that work?"

Eva shrugs, a playful smile on her lips. "We compromise. He cooks his tofu; I grill my steak. Love finds a way."

Bo wraps an arm around Eva's shoulders, pulling her close. "Exactly. Love finds a way."

Their banter is interrupted by Hank lighting the joint. Bo groans, stepping forward. "Dad, seriously. Not on the plane."

Hank looks at Bo with wide eyes, then at Rose, who is eagerly waiting for a hit. "Oh, right. Sorry, son."

Don snickers. "Imagine King Timos and Queen Rena getting a contact high. That would be a sight."

Eva tries to suppress her laughter but fails. "Let's not give them any ideas."

Rose pouts, stashing the joint back into her fanny pack. "Fine, but I still think the Queen might enjoy it."

Bo sighs, exasperated but amused. "Mom, you can't smoke weed in the palace."

Rose lifts her chin defiantly. "And why not? It's natural. The Queen might appreciate a little natural relaxation."

Eva rubs her stomach in circles, a secret smile plays on her lips. "That's not the only reason to avoid the hit."

The cabin falls silent, all eyes on her. Then on Bo. Eva takes Bo's hand and places it gently on her stomach and nods at Bo. "We're pregnant." They sing out in unison.

Cries of joy fill the cabin. Don and Greta rush forward and circle Bo and Eva in hugs. "Congratulations!" Greta exclaims, her eyes bright with excitement.

Rose and Hank beam with joy. "We're going to be grandparents!" Rose's voice is choked with emotion.

Hank's eyes are suspiciously wet. "Well done, son. Well done." He waves in the air to clear any residual and questionable clouds.

Bo looks at Eva and even his eyes shimmer. He leans in, pressing a tender kiss to her lips. "I love you." He whispers with thick emotion.

Eva smiles, her heart full. "And I love you."

Granola bars with the faint aroma of Hank's creation emit a unique blend of atmosphere. The touch of Bo's hand on her belly and the taste of his kiss, and the sound of their friends' laughter carry them over the Atlantic towards life's new horizon, with love, happiness, and new beginnings.

THE END.

COUNTESS WHO KISSED A COUNT

If you enjoyed reading **Countess Who Kissed a Count**, please consider giving it a review.

READ MORE BOOKS FROM **IreAnne Chambers**:
Majestic Estates Series:
Storm Chasers of Wentworth Hall.
Folly at Sausmarez Manor
Mystery at Harlaxton House
Wolfe of Toddington Peaks
Regency's British Empire Series:
Aphrodite Mine
Isle of My Man
Aliens of Extraordinary Ability Series:
Nightingale Song
Bollywood Bargain
Seasons Bliss Series:
Countess who Kissed a Count
One Man and a Babe

Find all books by IreAnne at:
www.IreAnneChambers.com
Join the The Cozy News for New Releases.

ABOUT THE AUTHOR

IREANNE CHAMBERS' BOOKS contain the spirit and tone of the traditional Regency with the promise of mystery, adventure, and mishap weaved in to create happy-ever-afters with plenty of fun and surprises along the way.

IreAnne looked to her Scottish and Irish heritage and discovered the name Eireann (Erin). Eire means Ireland in Gaelic and IreAnne was born.

IreAnne also enjoys writing poetry and song lyrics, but her love for the Regency romances of Jane Austen, filled with dashing heroes and feisty heroines, spurs her desire to write Fun, Cozy, Historicals, and Then Some...

As novelist and Nobel Prize winner Toni Morrison said, "If there's a book you really want to read, but it hasn't been written yet, then you must write it." IreAnne does just that.

Follow **IreAnne** here:

BookBub

Amazon

Goodreads

Instagram

Facebook

Pinterest

Twitter

Don't miss out!

Visit the website below and you can sign up to receive emails whenever IreAnne Chambers publishes a new book. There's no charge and no obligation.

https://books2read.com/r/B-A-FKKH-WXEEF

BOOKS 2 READ

Connecting independent readers to independent writers.

www.ingramcontent.com/pod-product-compliance
Lightning Source LLC
Chambersburg PA
CBHW020909180626
46816CB00007BA/2318